IT'S BEEN TOO LONG SINCE I'VE DANCED

BY DOTTIE FERRARA

Dedicated to:

Joe
Thank you for your encouragement, help, patience, and belief in me.

Maryanne
Thank you for your help and encouragement.

1941–1968

"What lies behind us and what lies before us are tiny matters compared to what lies within us."

—Ralph Waldo Emerson

Chapter 1

Billy Scott

Wednesday, December 11, 1940, 5:30 a.m.
Sara and Ray Baxter's Farm,
Charleston County, Missouri

The cries of pain coming from the house disturbed the quiet of the winter night and brought an uncommon restlessness to the barnyard residents. Roy's stooped shoulders heaved as he walked into the horse stables and slammed the door behind him. He buried his tanned weathered face in his hands and cried softly.

A young mare whinnied as if to say "What's wrong?"

Walking over to the mare's stall, he answered angrily, "Why did I let this happen? She is so damn young, too young to be havin'' a baby. I could kill that boy."

As if to comfort the man that took her into his confidence, the chestnut-colored mare nuzzled his shoulder.

Inside the farmhouse a girl whimpered in pain as an exhausting contraction slowly subsided.

"Okay, baby, with the next one you're gonna push as hard as you can, and this will be over in no time," came the

1

encouraging words of Sara as she placed a cool, wet cloth on the girl's head. Beads of sweat ran down the sides of the woman's face and onto the collar of her cotton printed dress. The frown lines in her face showed more worry than her words expressed. "Okay, baby, remember to push," she repeated.

Dr. Johnson, sitting on a stool between the girl's legs, with his hands readied to help the newborn into the world, waited for the next surge. Doc, as the locals called him, knew something the others didn't know. He knew that the girl's high blood pressure made it dangerous for her to deliver this large baby. He prayed that she could manage to birth this baby with the next couple of contractions.

The girl's low moans started slowly at first, then quickly rose in urgency in an uncontrollable need to release the pain through her cries. Suddenly, she let out a bloodcurdling scream that pierced the night's stillness with the sounds of anguish and seemed to shake the very foundation of the little house her family called home.

The woman by the bed yelled, "Push, Nell, push, push!"

The welcomed cries of a newborn filled the room. Sara and the young woman next to her clapped their hands with excitement, hugged, and exchanging words of relief.

Doc held up the wet newborn and cried out with joy, "Get them towels, woman, and wrap up this baby."

Sara reached for the warmed towels in the basket by the woodstove and gently wrapped the screaming infant. The baby's cries continued as the woman held it close and hurried into the kitchen.

The girl cried out with each stitch as Doc completed the delivery procedure. When finished, he reached over and patted the arm of the exhausted girl. "It's all right, sweetheart—you'll be fine now. You're now the momma of a big ol' boy."

Just then, the sound of the baby's loud cries came from the kitchen. Doc smiled and said, "He has all ten fingers and ten toes, and as you can tell, there is nothing wrong with his lungs."

As Doc smoothed the hair away from her cheeks and removed the damp cloth from her forehead, the exhausted girl murmured, "Thanks, Doc."

The women were huddled at the washbasin bathing the baby and talking happily about his blond hair, when all of a sudden the farmer burst through the back door of the porch and rushed into the kitchen. His large brown eyes darted around the room asking the questions his mouth couldn't form.

The tall woman answered the eyes, "She's fine, Ray. The baby is fine. Go see Nell."

Ray plopped down in the wooden kitchen chair and let out the breath that he had unnoticeably been holding in as he ran from the barn and into the house. "No, no, not yet!" he whispered, still trying to catch his breath.

"Please, Ray, we have a beautiful grandson," Sara said.

"Sara, I'm not ready yet!" he begged. He stood up, peeked around the kitchen door, and peered into the living quarters. With the newborn swaddled in a baby blanket, Sara moved closer to Ray.

When he turned around, she gently pushed the baby against her husband and said, "Ray, stop this and look at your beautiful grandson."

Looking down at Sara, he gazed into her smiling eyes, and with a deep sigh placed his long muscular arm around her shoulders. Moving the blanket from the sleeping infant, he gently touched the soft blond hair of his newborn grandson. With a crooked little smile, his face softened as he looked at the miracle in his wife's arms.

The doctor left the living room, and the younger woman slipped into the chair at Nell's bedside. She leaned down, kissed her pretty niece on the forehead, and whispered, "It's going to be alright, Nell. We will take care of you and the baby."

The girl opened her eyes slowly, "Aunt Marcy, is that you?"

Yes, dear, it's me. You're fine. It's almost morning. Rest now, and when you wake up you can hold your baby boy." Without saying another word, the exhausted Nell fell asleep.

The morning sun's rays came through the window, lighting Nell's face with a soft glow. The light roused her from a deep sleep, and for a few seconds she forgot where she was.

Rudely, the memory of thirty-eight hours of labor rushed back, and she shivered as if she was cold. Nell moved her hands over her breasts and down her body, letting them rest on her stomach. She sighed and thought, Yes it's over, really over.

A baby's cry came from the bedroom. Nell pulled the covers over her head and pretended to be asleep.

Sara came through the open door with the crying bundle in her arms. She whispered sweet words and rocked the baby gently as she walked over to Nell's bedside. "Are you ready to see what God brought to us?" The baby quieted.

Nell removed the blanket from her face and tried to lift herself up, but an unfamiliar pain surged through her body. She cried out as she flopped back against the pillow.

"Okay, sweetheart, you stay where you are. I'll lay the baby beside you and get another pillow to raise your head."

Gently, Sara placed the newborn on the bed and guided Nell's arms around the bundle until she felt that the baby was safe in the mother's awkward embrace.

Pulling back the soft blanket from the baby's face, Nell gasped as if surprised. "Is this it? Was this inside me all them months? Is this what all the fuss was about and made me have to quit school? Is this why people made fun of me?" Tears filled her brown eyes. The thing that she had hated for months began squirming and making funny grunting noises.

Its eyes opened; big chocolate-brown eyes looked back at Nell. The fifteen-year-old girl felt something unfamiliar stir inside her heart.

Doc came into the room and smiled as he approached mother and son. He felt thankful that all had turned out well with this delivery. At the bedside he softly said, "Nell, I must go into town and file a birth certificate; what are you going to call this big boy?"

"Billy Scott," replied Sara, coming into the room with pillows in her arms.

Doc looked quizzically at Nell. "Is that the name, Nell?" he asked.

Nell looked confused for a moment, then replied, "Yes, I guess it is."

Doc gave a cautious look toward Sara and asked, "I need to know the name of the daddy so we can put it on the birth certificate."

Sara grimaced and answered, "No father's name on the certificate. This baby will be a Baxter."

Nell's head bowed, and her long brown hair covered her face. A single tear rolled down her cheek and dropped softly on the forehead of the baby cradled in her arms.

A loud thump coming from the back of the house made Sara jump. She rushed out of the room and entered the back porch. There she found that Ray had lugged the scale from the barn onto the porch so he could weigh his grandson.

The next day while sitting around the dinner table Sara, Ray, and Marcy discussed the unreasonable fact that Billy Scott weighed over ten pounds. Sara was the first to make the statement that they all were thinking: "How in God's name could little Nell have delivered a baby that big?"

A hush fell over the room as they all said a private prayer of thanks.

Chapter 2

Tuesday, March 3, 1942
Sara and Ray Baxter's Farm

The toddler with striking blond hair slipped out the front door and onto the front porch of the small wood-framed house. Billy giggled as he made his way to the edge. He sat on his bottom and scooted down each step. After pulling himself up, he wobbled with unstable footing across the yard toward the trees. Brownie, the brown shepherd dog chained to an uncommonly large oak tree, stood up and wagged his tail wildly at the sight of the fifteen-month-old child heading his way.

Seeing Billy through the open door, Sara ran out onto the porch and yelled, "Billy Scott, you come back here. Where do you think you're going, you li'l rascal?"

She jumped off the porch, took four large steps, and scooped him up into her arms. The child laughed as Sara began to kiss him all over, making yum yum sounds as they headed back into the house.

Buster yelped franticly with disappointment at the loss of a playmate.

Gracie Lyn

Tuesday, March 3 1942
Albert and Miss Annie Meriwether's farm
Charleston County, Missouri

A little over thirty miles away from the toddler's failed escape, a farmer's young wife walked down a graveled road with a little suitcase in one hand. As most women would in the last days of pregnancy, she swayed from side to side from her heavy load.

Edna had walked down this road many times, but today she walked much slower, and the short distance between her house and her father in-law's farm seemed farther than ever before.

Her in-laws' barnyard teamed with life this evening. Milk cows waited in their stalls with udders full of milk, horses whinnied impatiently for their evening hay, and chickens casually pecked their way to the henhouse, where they would roost through the night. A golden-colored loose-limbed dog of unknown breed swaggered happily down the rutted driveway to greet Edna.

A short, plump woman with a pretty face and salt-and-pepper black hair came out of the house and stood on the front porch. Looking out toward the road, she saw Edna. Abruptly she hurried off the porch and down the rutted driveway.

Edna called out, "It's time, Miss Annie! I'm ready!"

The house Albert built just up the road away from the creek had two bedrooms, a tiny closet, a kitchen, a small dining room, a living room, and a room at the back of the house. This room was completely open, but covered with a screen, for sleeping during the hot summer nights.

Covering the inside walls were many layers of decorated flowered paper, and the floors were linoleum. Every few years, in an effort to keep her farmhouse clean and cheerful, Miss Annie ordered new wallpaper and linoleum from the Sears and Roebuck catalog. The wooden house was all gray and weathered on the outside except for the brick-red siding that covered the exterior walls. Large flat rocks placed in strategic locations under the frame of the house served as the foundation.

The house faced a large open area filled with huge oak trees and a graveled road. The "back" porch, which was really at the side of the house, faced the barnyard. The barn with hayloft, milking shed, and tractor shed sat a good distance from the house. The smokehouse sat at the back close to the end of the long back porch. About fifty yards from the house sat the very modern outhouse with a cement seat and septic tank. When the temperature dipped below zero, those fifty yards to the outhouse seemed like fifty miles.

Miss Annie and Brownie met Edna at the road. Miss Annie took the suitcase from her, and to steady Edna's steps, she placed her arm tightly around the wobbling young woman's waist. Happily, they walked and talked all the way up the driveway, across the yard, and into the house.

Gratefulness filled Edna's heart when she saw how well her mother-in-law and father-in-law had prepared their house for the baby's delivery. The bed with the feather mattress was in the living room a comfortable distance from the woodstove. Expecting a cold day and night, Albert had placed plenty of extra wood in the wood box. A big pot of water sat on the cooking stove ready for heating. Towels, sheets, and blankets lay neatly folded at the end of the bed waiting for the mother-to-be.

Edna noticed that on the little table by the bed Miss Annie had placed a small feather mattress, a soft warm blanket, and tiny baby gowns, all handmade from flour-sack material. Edna turned and faced Miss Annie and said, "Thank you."

After Miss Annie helped Edna change into a flannel nightgown and get in bed, she hurried to the milking shed behind the barn hoping to find Albert there. As she came around the corner of the barn, she bumped into him. Relieved, she said, "Oh, thank goodness you're here."

"Hey, woman, what are you doing?" he bellowed.

"Albert, you gotta go find William. Edna is in labor," Miss Annie exclaimed.

"Isn't he home?" Albert asked.

"Edna don't know where he's at. You gotta find him. She cain't have this baby by herself—she needs Doc McAdams now. She needs William to go get him," Miss Annie said in a hurried excitement.

Albert frowned. "I'll go get McAdams, then head up to the Stafford's' and see if William is roaming around up there. I swear if that boy is a sniffin' around Nadine again, I'm going to hit him up the side of the head."

William, riding his big black stallion, came thundering up the driveway just as Albert and Miss Annie came out from behind the barn.

Waving his arms frantically, Albert yelled to the young man on the horse, "Go get Doc McAdams; it's time. The baby is a coming!"

William pulled hard on Blackjack's reins, and the horse came to a jerking halt. Looking puzzled, he called out to Albert, "What?"

Albert yelled again, "The baby's a coming. Go get McAdams!"

William's piercing blue eyes became wide with startled understanding. "Tell Edna I'm on my way," he called back to Albert.

He kicked the stallion in the sides and pulled the reins to the left so hard that the horse reared up. His hooves pawed the air and came down, striking the ground with a thud. Like a flash, the man turned the wild-looking horse dynamically and heading back toward the road, sending rocks and gravel flying in all directions.

Tuesday, March 4, 1942, 9:30 am

Albert and William, sitting at the kitchen table, were arguing about William's lack of fidelity, when they heard the baby's cries coming from the living room.

William jumped up, hurried to the door, and waited. Soon Miss Annie entered with the baby wrapped in a receiving blanket. "William, it's a girl," she said. "Get the hot water from the kettle on the stove and pour it in that little dishpan on the sink."

"Add some cold water from the bucket there by the dishpan," she added.

Quickly he added cold water. Miss Annie tested the water with her elbow and found the temperature was just right. William, standing nearby, watched closely as Miss Annie held the baby in one arm and gently lowered her into the warm water. With a soft cloth, she washed what was left of the afterbirth from the tiny body. When finished, she wrapped the baby in a warmed blanket and handed the infant girl to William.

He took her cautiously into his arms. "What's wrong with her?" he asked as he held his daughter with the bruised and distorted face.

Miss Annie chuckled. "Oh, she's fine. She had a hard time being born, but tomorrow she will be all pink and beautiful—you wait and see. Come on; let's take her to see her momma."

Edna's sparkling brown eyes filled with tears as William carefully lay the sleeping baby in her arms. She leaned down, placed a soft gentle kiss on her baby's forehead, and said teasingly, "She's so ugly."

Miss Annie and Doctor McAdams smiled. William and Albert looked at each other quizzically and frowned. They just couldn't believe Edna said that about her new baby. They didn't understand that Edna was making a joke.

Dr. McAdams went to the table to fill out the birth certificate, saying, "I have to go to Jacksonville tomorrow. I'll file this birth notice at the courthouse."

Chuckling, he asked Edna, "What's this ugly child's name?"

Sleepily, she responded, "Grace Lyn."

Chapter 3

Saturday, September 23, 1945
William and Edna's Farm
Charleston County, Missouri

William lifted his giggling young daughter high above his head and brought her gently down onto the bare back of the large red horse. The small child's body bounced unsteadily as her daddy led the mare around the corral.

Excitedly, she coached, "Go, Daddy, go."

From the front porch of the weathered gray house, Edna called, "William, supper is on the table. Come and get it."

Edna crossed the porch and walked into the house, turned back, and pulled on the screened door to make sure it shut tightly.

Mumbling, Edna said, "Where is my flyswatter? Those darn flies are driving me plumb crazy." Picking up the swatter, she slowly walked around the room searching for the little black creatures. "Darn, where did they go? They disappear every time I have a flyswatter in my hand."

Walking in the front door with Gracie Jean in his arms, William asked, "Woman, you talking to yourself again?"

"Yes, but pay no mind. I'm just looking for those flies that snuck in the front door. Take Gracie over to the pump and wash her hands and face so we can eat supper before it gets cold."

As the sun set behind the adjacent woods, and the heat lessened to a comfortable temperature, the little family sat down to have their meal. On the dinner table covered with a yellow-flowered oilcloth Edna placed their supper of fried potatoes, cornbread, fried chicken, and green beans.

Their little house had one large room in the front and a partially enclosed back porch. On the left side of the large room was a bed, a chest of drawers, a cot, a heating stove, and a wood bin full of wood. On the right side of the room sat a counter with a washbasin and water pump. A crude shelf for dishes and pots and pans hung conspicuously above the washbasin. At the end on the counter near the front door sat a straight-back wooden chair and a three-foot-tall console radio. Near the back of the room was a small black wood-burning cooking stove, and in the middle of the room a small dinner table with three old wooden chairs. At the back of the house was an enclosed porch, a small table, and a galvanized washtub; this was considered the second room of the little house. The tub had two purposes: washing their clothing and bathing. The well sat just outside the back door.

The house sat back from the graveled road about thirty feet. In front of the porch, a bed of daisies struggled to survive in the hundred-degree heat of this Ozark summer. Across the road from the house, a small barn for milking and storing hay leaned a little to the left from the strong winds of the last tornado that had blown through the nearby countryside.

Mary looked around the room and frowned a little. "William, I've been thinking—"

"Oh, that's not good," William said with a grin.

"No, listen, I'm serious," Edna said. "Winter will be here before you know it, and this house is too cold for Gracie. She had two ear infections and pneumonia last winter. Doc McAdams said we had to find a way to get her to eat more and keep her warm."

"What can we do?" he asked. "This old house ain't worth fixin' up. Besides, next spring we're going to go to California as soon as they finish building Brother Jim's service station. I promised I would come and work for him."

"Will your brother put us up?" Edna asked

"Yes, until we can make a little money and find a place."

"Maybe we can go before the station is built and stay with him this winter?"

"No he ain't got that kind of room. We cain't stay for months," William answered, frowning.

"We have to think of something; the baby cain't stay in this old house another winter. I'm gonna ask Albert and Miss Annie if we can hole up there for a couple months," Edna said flatly.

"Go ahead, I don't think they'll mind; they're crazy about Gracie Lyn, and you're a big help to Miss Annie. I don't see how she makes it working in the fields all day, caring for her hogs and chickens after that, and still puts a decent meal on the table."

"She's one of a kind, that's for sure," Edna said, smiling at the thought of her quiet and thoughtful mother-in-law.

With their own private thoughts of the future, Edna and William ate in silence, until Gracie Lyn giggled as she dropped pieces of chicken into Blackie's open mouth— William's hound dog.

"That dog is hiding under the table. How did he get in this house? Gracie Lyn Jean, stop giving that dog good chicken. Blackie, you get yourself to the back porch," Edna said loudly.

Giggling, Gracie Lyn dropped another piece of chicken onto the floor. Blackie grabbed it and bolted out of the room.

Chapter 4

Monday, October 21, 1946
William and Edna's Apartment
San Jose, CA

Looking out the window, Gracie Lyn watched as the three children came out of the neighboring cluster of apartments and gathered in the courtyard. Chattering among themselves, they continued toward the sidewalk in front of the buildings.

"Where are all those kids going?" Gracie Lyn asked.

Walking to the window to see what Gracie Lyn was talking about, Edna replied, "They're going to school."

Jumping down from the sofa, Gracie Lyn looked up at her mother. "I wanna go to school too."

"Sorry, baby you're too young. You cain't go until next year," Edna, answered.

"I wanna go to school too! Please, Mama, please! I wanna go too!

"Gracie Lyn, school is where big kids go and sit in a room with a teacher and learn how to do things like read and write. I think you must be five to go to school."

"I'm almost five, Mommy; I'm almost five! I can write my name, I know my numbers and can read all the stories in my Mother Goose book. Please mommy, please," she said, wrapping her arms around Edna's legs and starting to cry.

That evening, still in his service station uniform, William sat at the kitchen table reading the evening paper. Edna approached, pulled out a chair, and sat down. She sat there quietly, hands folded together on the table, waiting for William to look up and acknowledge her.

"What?" William asked.

"Gracie wants to go to school," Edna answered.

"I don't think she is old enough," he said.

"She saw the children in the complex going to school this morning, and she began to cry and beg me to let her go. I think she's curious since she's never had friends her own age. She knows her ABCs and numbers better than most six-year-olds do, and she'll be five in a few months. I've decided to go to the school tomorrow and see if they'll let her enroll," Edna said.

"Well, you can go ask," William said, looking back at his newspaper.

Two weeks later:

Edna placed the mashed potatoes on the table next to the fried chicken. Turning to the counter, she picked up the pitcher of ice tea and called to William, "Supper is ready."

Coming into the room, William asked, "Where is Gracie Lyn? Is she in her room?"

"No, she went shopping with your sister. She should be home anytime. Gracie Lyn came home from her first day at school and told me that she met a chocolate girl and a girl with blue hair," Edna said, grinning at William.

"What?" William exclaimed.

"She came home very excited, and the first thing she said was that a girl sitting beside her in class was chocolate and another girl she played with at recess had blue hair.

William, Gracie Lyn has never seen a colored person before, and I'm guessing the other girl was an I-talian or Mexican," Edna said.

William started laughing.

"William, it's not funny. Our little daughter has been on the farm her whole life. We never took her any place where people are different from us. She doesn't know anything."

"What's there to know? She'll find out while she's in school. Besides, she went to Garberville and Newark a few time with me and Pa," he said, still smiling.

"Yes, but I guess she didn't see any coloreds or she would know that there are such a thing as colored people. If she had, she wouldn't have been so surprised to see one in her class." Edna said.

"You're right—there ain't many coloreds in Garberville."

The front door opened with a bang. The slender little girl ran in. Going straight to her daddy, she yelled, "Daddy, Daddy, guess what? There is a chocolate girl in my school, and she sits rights next to me. I like school. There are lots of kids, and we play, and draw, and swing on swings, and everything. We have to take naps too. I didn't go to sleep— the chocolate girl was right next to me, and I like looking at her. She is different. She is pretty and nice. She has pigtails and pretty eyelashes. I think she is a special princess or something."

William smiled and looked up at Edna. She turned, wiped her hands on the apron tied around her waist, and walked to the kitchen laughing, "That girl sure does have an imagination."

A week later:

Edna smoothed her cotton flowered dress with the palm of her hands. Her back rigid against the wood chair as she waited in the grammar school's office for the principal to return. Miss Marshall, the principal, had left the office and said she would be back in a minute, but that minute had turned into five. Edna was already anxious to find out why the principal wanted her to come to the office, and this waiting wasn't making it easier. The letter she'd received said nothing about a problem, and the principal had said nothing about it before she walked out.

Edna left Gracie Lyn sitting on a bench outside the office and was just about to get up and go see if she was alright, when the door opened and the principal walked in with a very tall frowning Negro woman.

"Mrs. Meriwether, this is Mrs. Williams. I ask you to come in today because Mrs. Williams has a complaint against Gracie Lyn."

"What? What? What did Gracie Lyn do?" Edna asked.

"That girl of yours been staring at my Jasmine so much it's freaking her out. She says that your girl follows her around and won't leave her alone. She said she tries to touch her skin and touch her hair and Jasmine tells her no, but she keeps trying," Mrs. Williams said angrily.

"Oh my goodness, y'all don't understand. Gracie Lyn thinks Jasmine is beautiful and a princess, and . . . and," Edna stammered. "She thinks she has chocolate skin. She ain't never seen a Negro person before. We lived on a farm in the Ozarks, and there ain't no colored people around our part of the country. She means no harm. I'm so sorry if she upset your little girl. I'll talk to her, I'll explain what she's doing is wrong."

Mrs. Williams muffled a laugh and said, "Why, honey, I thought your little girl was crazy or something. I didn't know she liked my Jasmine. I'll talk to my girl too, and yes, she is so sweet sometimes I think she is made out of chocolate." Laughing, Mrs. Williams stood and walked over to Edna.

Edna stood. Mrs. Williams reached out to shake Edna's hand. Edna took her hand and said, "I'm so sorry. I'll talk to Gracie Lyn."

"Oh, honey, just get her to stop following Jasmine, and I'll explain to her what you told me, and everything will be fine," Mrs. Williams said, still chuckling.

Suddenly, children's happy voices came from the hallway outside the office. The principal got up, came around the desk, and opened the door. The mothers followed. The three women stood in the open doorway smiling at what they saw. There on the bench Gracie Lyn and Jasmine were playing patty–cake.

Miss Marshall turned to the mothers and said, "Ladies, I think everything going to be alright."

Thursday, December 18, 1947
Nell and Larry Parker's Home
River City, Missouri

The giggling girl's blond locks bounced as she ran around and around the yard with a small spotted hound puppy nipping at her heels. Stretched out on the porch swing, deep in thought, Billy paid no attention to his little sister and the puppy. Christmas vacation was starting in a few days, and he was trying to figure out he could hide and not go to school. The Casey brothers bullied him every day, and he didn't know what to do to make them stop.

"They push me and shove me and call me 'pretty boy.' They are so mean. MaMaw says I'm a pretty boy, but she smiles when she says it. Tommy and Buddy don't smile— they push me and laugh," Billy said out loud.

"Billy Scott," a loud voice came from beyond the screen door.

Startled and afraid that his mom heard his comments, Billy jumped out of the porch swing and called out, "I'm here on the porch."

The screen door opened, and his mother called to the little girl, "Carol, come in this house right now. It's too cold to be playing outside. Cain't you see the icicles on them trees? I don't need you catching a cold here just before Christmas."

The little girl still giggling ran toward the house and up the steps with the puppy close behind. She pushed past Billy and entered the front door. The boy and the puppy both tried to enter at the same time, but Nell stepped in between the two and said, "No, puppy, you ain't coming in this house."

She pushed the young dog back with her foot, grabbed Billy by his collar, pulled him into the room, and closed the door. Once inside Nell gave him a loving hug. When Billy started to squirm, she turned him around and gently slapped his bottom.

Inside the warm house, the Christmas tree lights gave the normally dreary living room a cheerful glow. The sweet smell of pecan pies baking in the kitchen made Billy's mouth water in anticipation.

He walked into the kitchen and asked, "Can I make something too?"

"Sorry, baby, I'm too busy right now. I don't want you underfoot while I'm baking." His mother smiled with the reply.

Frowning at the dismissal, Billy thought, MaMaw is making cookies, and she always lets me stand on the stool at the table and help her.

Billy asked politely, "Mommy, can I go to MaMaw's?"

"Go ahead and go, but you cain't spend the night tonight. I want you back here in two hours. Larry will be home at five thirty, and we'll have dinner. I'm making your favorite—chicken and dumplin's. Billy, don't you slam the door on your way out."

"Okay, Mommy," Billy yelled as he zipped through the living room and out the front door. A loud bang came from the screen door as it slammed shut.

He ran all the way down the road to his grandparents' house. Reaching their porch, he jumped two steps at a time, and skipped all the way to the front door. Opening the door without knocking, he shouted, "MaMaw?"

From somewhere in the back of the house his grandmother replied, "Is that my boy coming to visit?"

They found each other in the hallway. The tall, slender woman reached down, pulled the boy into her arms, and swung him around and around while hugging him gently. Lowering him to the floor, she said, "Come on in the kitchen and help me make some of them coconut cookies that you like so well."

Chapter 5

Sunday, August 31, 1947
William and Edna Farm
Charleston County, Missouri

"I have a big surprise for you," William said. "Run in the house and tell your mom we're leaving."

Gracie Lyn hurried toward the house, opened the front door, and excitedly yelled, "Mommy, daddy is taking me someplace in the truck."

Returning to the truck she ask enthusiastically, "Where are we going, Daddy?".

"I told you it's a surprise," William answered. "Hop in the truck." He opened the door.

Gracie Lyn crawled into the truck and got on her knees with her legs folded under her so she could see out the windshield. "Where are we going, Daddy?" she asked again.

"Hold your horses!" William said, laughing.

Pulling into the long rutted driveway, William's truck began to bounce and dip, sending Gracie Lyn into the floor. William stopped abruptly. "Are you alright?" he asked, grabbing her by the arm.

"Sure," she said, laughing while climbing into the seat.

Looking out the window at a corral with five or six horses, William said, "See that little red mare off to the side there, the one by herself?"

"Yes." Before William could say another word Gracie Lyn exclaimed, "You bought me a horse. You bought me a horse!"

William smiled. "Sure did, kiddo!" as he pulled the truck up to the horse barn.

William pulled the truck into the driveway of their house and parked by the water well near the barnyard gate.

Gracie Lyn jumped out of the truck and slammed the door.

"Wait, Gracie Lyn! You let me tell your momma that I bought a horse. Alright?"

"Yes, Daddy," Gracie Lyn answered.

William opened the screened door and yelled, "Edna, we're home,"

From the kitchen Edna answered, "I'm in the kitchen."

Gracie Lyn pushed her way past her tall daddy and ran toward the kitchen yelling excitedly, "Mommy, Mommy, Daddy bought me a horse."

Edna came from the kitchen, meeting Gracie Lyn halfway into the living room, "William, what did you do? Gracie Lyn is only five. Her cain't be ridding no horse by herself. She's too little. Her cain't even get on one by herself."

"Edna, I think she will surprise you. She loves to be on a horse, and this horse is a very small mare. She's eighteen, but healthy and has good teeth and legs."

"And she mine all mine," Gracie Lyn added, jumping up and down, clapping her hands with delight. "I'm gonna name her Dolly. Dolly the horse."

Edna walked away shaking her head.

Saturday, December 21, 1947

Edna sat on the floor in front of the brightly lit Christmas tree singing to herself as she wrapped the baby doll that she bought from the Sears and Roebuck catalog. She turned and smiled at a small pink doll bed that sat in the corner of the room. Edna was pleased with the bed that she made out of an old wood crate. She was especially proud of the sheets, blanket, and a mattress, which she made by hand, using flour sacks and sterilized chicken feathers.

When she finished the wrapping task, she said to herself, "Those flour sacks sure do come in handy."

"What are you mumbling about, woman?" William asked as he entered the room.

"Oh, I was thinking about the printed flour sacks Miss Annie gave me and how many pretty things I made out of them," she answered.

As William approached, he stuck out his hand and showed her a bright red toy truck and tractor. "Don't forget to wrap these. Gracie Lyn has been begging me for these since her birthday. I swear, sometimes that child don't know if she is a boy or girl," he teased.

"She's a tomboy." Edna smiled.

"What's a tomboy?" he asked.

"A girl that likes to play outside in the ditch with a truck and tractor as much as she likes to play Mommy with a baby doll," she answered. "You know, William, she likes riding that horse more than anything else, but I think she is too young to go off riding all by herself the way she does. Do you know any other five-year-old girls running around these hills on a horse?"

"Oh, Edna, she can handle that horse better than she can walk. Dolly is good with her and does whatever she says. But, I'm telling you this, if she doesn't stop running Dolly like a bat out of hell, I'm going to take that little mare away from her. Dolly turned twenty last summer; she's too old to be running like that."

"Please don't do that. Gracie Lyn loves that horse so much. I'll have a talk with her about it again, and I'll tell her she needs to stay close to the farm instead of going off in the hills."

Edna jumped when she heard the sound of horse hooves coming down the driveway fast and hard. Quickly she moved the wrapped doll, blankets, and crib behind the tree.

"There's that little jug-head right now," William announced as he rushed out the front door expecting to find the twenty-year-old Dolly sweating from running down the hill again. Instead, he found the five-year-old Gracie Lyn sitting bareback on the little horse, no sweat anywhere in sight.

"Oh, Daddy, I didn't run Dolly—she ran down the driveway by herself. I couldn't stop her. Honest," Gracie Lyn said, her brown eyes pleading for William to believe her.

"Okay, but I'm glad you didn't, because I've decided that if I catch you running her again I'll take her away and put her in the Staffords' pasture," he warned.

Gracie Lyn grimaced. Her eyes closed tightly as she reached down and wrapped her arms around Dolly's neck. "No, Daddy, please, I won't run her again," she begged.

"It's a good thing, because I want to breed her, and she won't be able to carry a colt if she's lame." Taking the reins, William led the horse into the barnyard. Reaching up and helping Gracie Lyn from Dolly's back, he asked, "Do you want to go opossum hunting with me tonight? There's a two dollar bounty on them hides."

"Sure, Daddy," she said, "Do I have to carry the sack with the dead opossum again?"

"Of course, that's your job," William answered with a grin.

Chapter 6

Tuesday, June 1, 1948
Nell and Larry's Home

Billy reached for his schoolbooks sitting on the little table by the front door and called out to his mother in the kitchen, "Mommy, the bus is coming."

"Okay, baby, don't you go missing it again," she replied.

Billy slipped outside onto the porch and ran down the steps. The thought of riding on the school bus today had his heart thumping wildly. He knew the minute he stepped on the bus the Casey brothers would start picking on him again. Sometimes when he found a seat next to the bus driver they would leave him alone, but if he sat in the back, they bullied him all the way to school. Billy being small for his age—surprisingly so, considering his size at birth—was a sure target for the tormenters. However, today Billy had a plan. He wouldn't go to school. There were only two weeks left until summer vacation, and he decided to hide out every day until then.

As soon as Billy slipped around the corner of the house and made his way to his hiding place behind the wooden storage shed, he began to feel a sense of relief. A stack of lumber leaning against the back wall of the shed, with a small opening just the right size for a little boy, made a perfect place to hide from a world that seemed oppressive. He'd built this cozy fort during the last summer vacation. He placed old burlap sacks on the ground and brought an old blanket and pillow from the house for comfort when it was cool.

Smoked ham and vegetables that had been canned last fall were stored in the little shed. No one entered the shed until dinnertime, and no one ever came around to the back. Billy felt safe in his private hideaway.

Once inside he sat still and listened for the school bus to stop at the mailbox. The bus arrived on schedule. He waited until he heard the grind of the gears as the bus continued down the country road taking his classmates, as well as the bullies, to school. Now he could relax.

He pulled biscuits and fatback from one pocket, dried corn from another, and placed them in the corner near his pillow.

Billy looked through the fort's small opening and watched the chickens search for food. He always found them fascinating. The roosters pranced around, clucking loudly as if they were telling the hens what to do. The hens busily pecked at the ground as if the roosters didn't exist. The roosters would periodically chase one of the hens as if to say, "How dare you ignore me." Billy found that if he placed bits of corn at the entrance to the fort, the hens would cautiously come closer. If he sat quietly with corn in his hand, eventually one or two would venture into his fort and peck at the corn.

Peacefully the day went by while Billy talked to the chickens, took a nap, and ate his biscuits and fatback. He was happy hiding in his fort while the rest of the people in world carried out their day.

Billy heard the bus coming down the road long before it came to his stop. He jumped up and peeked out the opening to see if anyone was around. Nell, busy taking down the wash from the clothesline on the other side of the house, didn't see the small boy that slipped around the corner of the house and to the front yard. Billy knew that she couldn't see him hiding behind the large oak tree near the bus stop. His plan was to hop out as soon as the bus stopped and the doors opened. His mother would think he had just arrived home from school with the other children in the neighborhood.

The bus pulled up to the curb, and the Casey brothers saw the little boy behind the tree. They begin to giggle and point at Billy. When the doors to the bus swung open to let other children get off, Buddy, the oldest, jumped down onto the steps, pointed at Billy, and yelled, "There he is. There's Billy the bastard! Billy Scott the bastard. Ha-ha. Why didn't you go to school today, bastard—you too dumb?"

"Get back inside this bus, you little scoundrel," yelled the bus driver.

Buddy stepped back into the bus while still chanting his cruel words. This young bully was responsible for Billy's pain that fateful day, and for the pain he carried with him for the rest of his life. The bully never knew the damage he did not only to Billy but also to everyone in Billy's future. Billy never stopped feeling like a bastard.

Billy burst in the front door and slammed it so hard that Sara jumped at the sound of such a noise. Getting up from her kitchen chair she called out, "Who in the world a making such a racket?"

Before she opened the door into the living room, she called out, "Billy Scott, is that you?"

There was no answer, only sobbing. Quickly she opened the door and saw Billy lying on the floor. She ran to him, frantically thinking he was injured.

"What's wrong, Billy? Are you hurt?"

"No, No, MaMaw, its Buddy—he called me a bastard. He always hits me and calls me names."

Stunned silent, Sara pulled the sobbing boy into her arms and started rocking back and forth. She felt his stinging hot tears on her face as she tried to soothe the child's pain with her kisses. She always worried that this might happen someday, and knew that his age would determine how much of the truth she could give him.

Oh my God, why did that boy say that? Who has been talking around town? she thought.

Billy pulled his head away from Sara's shoulder and looked at her with red tearful eyes. "Why'd he say that, MaMaw?"

"Well, Son, now that this has been said, I guess I had better explain it to you. Let's go in the kitchen, and I'll get you some milk and cookies and we'll have ourselves a little talk."

Sitting in the chair with a cookie in one hand and a glass of milk in the other, Billy looked at his grandmother with wide-eyed anticipation of what secret she was about to tell him. She started slowly, trying to figure out as she went just how much he should know. She figured that eventually he would hear all the truth, but right now he was just too young to understand.

"Billy, you are not a bastard. A bastard is someone that ain't got no daddy. You got a daddy. Larry is your daddy. He's not your real daddy because your real daddy is no good, but you got a daddy, and it's Larry. When you're older we can talk again, and you'll understand."

Confused, Billy looked up at his grandmother and asked, "My real daddy is a bad man? My daddy is no good?"

"That's right, Son. Your real daddy is no good."

"MaMaw, am I no good too?"

Sara jumped up and took the boy into her arms, "Oh, Billy Scott, you are good. You are the best boy in the world.

Chapter 7

Friday, September 24, 1948
Garberville Grammar School,
Garberville, Missouri

Billy's face beamed with happiness as he waited anxiously for his ride home. His life had changed abruptly after Buddy's bastard remarks at the bus stop. He liked that his family had moved into Jacksonville, and he liked that he lived far away from the boys that had picked on him and hurt his feelings. He especially liked that sometimes Uncle Bobby gave him a ride to and from his new school. This morning Uncle Bobby told him that because he was a special boy he was going to pick him up after school and take him to the Dairy Queen for a chocolate-dipped ice cream.

Sitting on the schoolhouse steps, Billy jumped up when he heard the unmistakable loud engine of Bobby's truck coming down the street. He ran to the curb to wait, waving his thin arms frantically as if Bobby couldn't see him. The truck swerved much too close to Billy as it came to a jerking halt. Bobby jumped out of the truck, ran around to the passenger side, and yanked opened the passenger side door.

"This old door won't open half of the time," he announced. "I reckon I need to get that fixed one of these days."

He grabbed the boy around the waist with one arm, placed Billy in the seat, and slammed the door shut.

"Uncle Bobby, are we going to get some ice cream?" Billy asked timidly.

"We sure are, boy. It's so dang hot today I'm thinking we should go for a swim too."

Billy's eyes opened wide. "I don't have a swimming suit here."

"Oh heck, Billy, we're men—we don't need no swimming suit. Wouldn't you like to go have a nice cool swim? I know a place on the river that's great for swimming, and no one else knows about it. We can cool off, and there won't be anyone around to care if we have a swimming suit or not. Wanna go?"

"Is it okay with Mommy?" Billy asked.

"Sure it is. Heeeerrrre we go, first ice cream and then cooling off." Bobby's truck lurched into the street as Bobby stepped hard on the gas.

Nell and Larry Home,
Garberville
Later that night:

Billy slipped out from under the lightweight quilt and onto the rough wood floor. He couldn't sleep. He tiptoed to the bedroom window, opened it, and climbed out quietly. The full moon cast spooky shadows around the yard. Billy wasn't afraid of spooks. He went out at night many times and found the dark was his friend. He could think about things without someone constantly asking him why he was being so quiet. The only thing that made him afraid was the possibility of Larry catching him sneaking out. If that happened there would be a scolding or maybe a spanking.

Hurrying to the backyard, he entered his new hiding place behind the old garage and wrapped the blanket around his shoulders. He began to shiver, not from being cold but from the anxiety around the troubling events of the afternoon swim.

"I must be bad like my daddy," he said tearfully. His whispers blended into the eerie sounds of the night. "Uncle Bobby said what happened ain't being bad, but if it ain't, why can't I tell? I liked it when he hugged me and rubbed me. He told me that he loves me and that being a bastard made me special. He told me that I could be his special boy. Maybe what we did was bad. Maybe that's what MaMaw meant when she said that my real daddy was a bad man." Wiping tears away with the sleeve of his pajama top, the young boy stammered, "Maybe I'm bad too, like my daddy?"

Chapter 8

Friday, September 24, 1948
Lawrence Grammar School,
Lawrence, Missouri

Listening intently, Gracie Lyn lay on the floor within the half circle of children while the teacher told the story of a young woman's adventure in the jungles of Africa. She loved this story of the jungle and the princess, and she loved her beautiful young teacher. Miss Malone didn't read a line from a book but created the story from her imagination. Every afternoon during rest time, the children lay on their pallets mesmerized by her stories. It became the best part of the day for the students as well as the teacher.

"The princess rested on the soft moss and fell fast asleep. The apes moved quietly out of the jungle and slowly crawled close to the young woman. They were curious. Never had they seen anything so beautiful. They gathered around the sleeping beauty, being careful not to make a sound and wake her."

Rising from her chair, Miss Malone abruptly announced, "That's all for today, children. We must work on our printing this afternoon."

Gracie Lyn jumped up and ran to the teacher. Enthusiastically she asked, "Can you tell us more of the story after the printing?"

"Not today, Gracie Lyn—we have work to do," Miss Malone, answered.

Jumping up and down excitedly, Gracie Lyn continued to beg, "Please, please, please!"

"No, I said no more today. I'll tell you more of the story on Monday," said Miss Malone firmly.

Pouting and hanging her head, Gracie Lyn listlessly made her way to her desk and plopped down.

The school bell rang announcing the end of the day. Gracie Lyn, in line with the other students, filed out of the classroom and onto the school bus for the ride home. She slid into the seat next to the window. Her friend and neighbor Gloria Lyn sat next to her.

It was late afternoon and just about time for the creatures of the woods to come out of hiding and look for their evening meal. As the bus traveled down the graveled road, Gracie Lyn gazed out the window admiring the countryside. Sometimes when a deer or rabbit would make an appearance near the road she would clap her hands together excitedly from sheer delight of the sighting.

After several miles, she turned to her friend Gloria Lyn and said seriously, "I'm going to write stories when I grow up! I'm going to write about animals and trees. I love animals and I love trees!"

As the bus pulled up to the farmhouse, Gracie Lyn jumped out of her seat and waited at the door. Excited about her new idea of writing stories, she wanted to tell her mother this special news. Once the doors finally opened, she burst out and ran up the driveway as fast as her skinny little legs would carry her. She rushed through the front door and ran into the living room, but quickly halted before reaching her mother. Edna sat in the living room chair by the open window, her face red and swollen from crying.

"What's wrong, mommy?" Gracie Lyn gasped.

"I just had some bad news, sweetheart. Don't worry, it's okay. Go out to the chicken house and get me some eggs. I need them for dinner." Gracie Lyn, worrying that there was something terrible wrong again, walked up to her mama and gave her a hug.

"Go on, honey—get me some eggs," her mama pleaded as she deliberately pushed her away.

After gathering a few eggs, Gracie Lyn lingered in the barnyard to watch the kid goats play in the field. Running in one direction and then another, the kids jumped and kicked up their hooves as if delighted to be alive. She smiled at the beauty of this small gesture of joy. Quickly the smile faded as she remembered why she dreaded going back into the house. She witnessed her mother crying often and always felt helpless. Now she tried to avoid her when it happened.

Taking a deep breath, she turned and walked through the gate toward the house. Opening the screen door quietly, she entered the back porch, walked over to the table near the water well, and laid the eggs in a basket next to the empty water bucket. Staring at the dented galvanized bucket sitting on the table, she whispered, "I ain't gonna fill that bucket like I'm supposed to even if it makes Daddy mad. I bet it was him that made Mommy cry again." Leaving the back porch, she walked hurriedly toward the barnyard not noticing the truck that had just pulled into the driveway.

Gracie Lyn climbed the ladder to the barn loft window and entered. Slowly she crawled to the mound of hay in the corner, reached deeply into the dusty straw, and gently pulled out a tiny kitten from its warm and comfortable bed. Finding a suitable place to sit, she placed the mewing kitten in her lap and proceeded to gathered another kitten, and then another, until her lap was filled with squirming, mewing kittens. Holding the soft cuddly balls of fur always made her feel better.

A loud ranting from the driveway below startled her. She jumped up, scattering kittens onto the hay. She went to the loft window and looked out.

At that very moment she saw her Daddy's fist go flying into the open window of a blue Ford pickup hitting the face of the man sitting behind the steering wheel. Even from this distance she could see the blood fly out of the stranger's nose and splash against the windshield on the inside of the truck.

The truck motor roared as it backed out of driveway fast and recklessly, almost going into the ditch next to the gravel road before speeding out of sight. Her daddy held his hand awkwardly up in the air with a noticeable amount of blood running down his arm as he walked to the house and stormed through stormed throughentered the front door.Hastily she climbed down the ladder and ran out of the barnyard. Even before she reached the house, she could hear her daddy yelling at her Mommy. At the porch, she stopped and waited by the door.

"I know the only reason Charles came to this house was because he thought I was gone and he wanted you. I've seen the way he looks at you when we're in town. He follows you around like a puppy," William yelled.

"William, that's not true. He doesn't even try to talk to me," Edna sobbed.

"You're lying!" William yelled louder. "You must have been flirting with him for him to come all the way out here."

Edna cried out, "What do you care? You didn't even come home last night. You were out at the Stanfords' whoring around Nadine."

"Don't you mind where I was. You just be a wife and stop flirting with all them men."

"William, I never flirt, you know that. You are the one that flirts with everything with a skirt on," Edna whimpered.

Just as William's bloodied hand raised high in the air ready to slap Edna's face, Gracie Lyn screamed, "Don't you hit my mommy!" as she came running in the front door.

William turned in disbelief that his little daughter had witnessed his rage again. Face red with anger and frustration, he quickly left the room. Edna buried her face in her hands and sobbed.

Not knowing what to do next, Gracie Lyn ran back out into the yard. She went out the back gate into the barnyard and walked slowly down the wagon path into the field behind the smokehouse. When she was far enough away that she couldn't see the house anymore she sat on the ground and cried, "Why is Daddy so mean? Sometimes he is so happy and funny, and then he gets mean. He tells Mommy he loves her—I hear it all the time. So why does he make her cry so much?"

The joy Gracie Lyn felt on the school bus and her dream of writing stories were gone. In its place confusion and sadness had found a home.

Chapter 9

Tuesday, June 12, 1951
Sara and Ray Baxter's Home

Handkerchief in hand, mopping the sweat from his face and neck, Ray entered the house from the back porch.

"Hot damn, it must be a hundred and ten degrees out there today," he declared as he walked into the kitchen and kissed Sara on the cheek.

Sara didn't reply. She opened the refrigerator door and pulled out a pitcher of sweet tea and sat it on the kitchen table. After taking a glass from the cupboard, she filled it with tea and handed it to Ray. With a sigh, Sara plopped down into the chair at the end of the table.

"What's wrong with you today? You ain't been yourself all day," Ray said as he pulled the chair out from under the table and sat down across from Sara.

"Bobby took Billy out swimming again today, and they haven't come back yet. He spends a lot of time with that boy. Billy doesn't have any time to make friends because Bobby keeps him too busy," Sara said.

"Don't worry, Bobby is doing good by the boy. Larry doesn't spend much time with him, and it's good that his uncle shows him how to grow up to be a man."

"I know, but you would think Bobby would spend more time with men his own age. When Billy comes home from his day with Bobby, he don't talk much, and then he disappears for hours. Nell don't worry none. She's glad Billy has someone to keep him busy. Bobby won't take Carol when they go swimming, and she cries her eyes out every time they take off."

"You're just a worrywart, and you think too much," Ray said as he reached out across the table and patted her hand.

Sounds of laughter came from the front porch. Sara got up from the chair and went to the window to look out.

"Well, I'll be darned. Billy's sitting on the swing with that Smith boy. It looks like he went swimming with Billy and Bobby. Guess Billy made a new friend after all, and I was worried for no good reason."

"Well, woman, that's your job, ain't it?" Ray chimed in with a grin.

Smiling at Ray, Sara said, "You hush up, somebody has to think about what's going on around here," as she pulled a platter of cookies from the white china cabinet near the window. "You boys want some cookies and milk?" she called from the open window.

"See, I told you MaMaw had cookies," Billy said quietly to the freckle-faced boy with red hair sitting next to him on the swing.

Billy entered the house with Sam right behind him and yelled, "Mom, can Sam stay and eat supper?"

"Okay, if it's alright with his mother," Nell called out from the kitchen.

"We already asked her, and she said it's okay," Billy answered.

"We're having chicken and dumplings, your favorite."

Leaning into his friend's ear, Billy whispered, "I knew that." Then to his mother he called, "We're going to the backyard. I want to show Sam my chickens."

"Okay, I'll call you when dinner is on the table."

Sitting on the ground with their backs up against the henhouse, the two boys watched while the chickens pecked randomly at the ground. "What are they eating?" Sam asked.

"I don't know—bugs, gravel, and maybe seeds. They eat gravel for their gullet. That's the way they digest their food," Billy answered, sounding knowledgeable.

"What? They eat rocks? A gullet—what's that?" Sam replied.

"It's a thing in their throat. It helps them digest their food. I don't really know how. I just read it in my book about birds," Billy admitted.

"Your uncle Bobby is strange," Sam said suddenly.

"Strange? Why is he strange?" Billy said as the top of his ears immediately begin to feel warm and his cheeks flushed.

"I don't know. He touched me a lot and always had a funny look on his face."

Pretending to defend Bobby, Billy said, "He just likes to be friendly. I don't think he meant anything by it."

"I don't think I want to go swimming with him again." Sam frowned at the thought of Bobby helping him swim.

"Yeah, me too; we hardly ever go swimming anyway," Billy said.

"What'cha doing tomorrow?"

"Nuttin', I guess," Billy said.

"You can come to my house, and I can show you my train set. It's laid out all over my room."

"Wow, that sounds like fun," Billy said excitedly.

Later that night, Billy lay in his bed thinking about the day and how much fun he had with his new friend Sam. "Sam is the nicest boy in my class. He invited me to go to his pop's restaurant and have ice cream after school on Monday, but Bobby is supposed to pick me up after school. He'll be mad if he finds out that I went with Sam." Billy frowned. "I told him not to do anything funny to Sam. I saw him trying. He didn't fool me. I know what he was thinking. I'm glad Sam doesn't want to go swimming with him again. Bobby is going to be mad at me, but I like having Sam as a friend, and there's nothing Bobby can do about that."

Chapter 10

Tuesday, June 12, 1951
William and Edna's Farmhouse

Lying on her bed facing the window, Gracie Lyn could look out and see the gravel road and the entrance to the driveway. She jerked her head up for a better view every time she heard a truck coming down the road. It was late afternoon, and what seemed like many hours had passed since her daddy went to the Jacksonville bus stop to pick up her uncle Johnny Lynn. Hearing the soothing sound of her mother softly singing, Gracie Lyn turned her head and looked through the kitchen door. Standing at the old wood cooking stove, Edna busily dipped the pastry dough into the hot oil. Puffed-up sugar-glazed donuts were to be a special surprise for Johnny Lynn when he arrived.

Johnny, Edna's youngest brother, always spent summer vacations at their farm. He was only a few years older than Gracie Lyn, and they were more like brother and sister than uncle and niece.

When Gracie Lyn's eyelids grew heavy with the need to sleep, she called out to her mom, "I'm tired of waiting, Mommy. I'm sleepy."

"I thought you looked a little peaked this afternoon. You may have a little fever. Go ahead and take a nap, and I'll wake you when Johnny gets here," Edna called out to the little girl curled up in a fetal position next to the open window.

Just a few minutes later William's truck pulled into the driveway. Edna walked to the bedroom door and looked at the sleeping child. She decided to let her sleep.

Five days later, Doc McAdams blue eyes twinkled with delight as he gave Edna's arm a little squeeze.

"Her fever broke about an hour ago, and she should be up and around in a few days, but with a fever that high she'll be weak for quite a while," he said professionally.

Gracie Lyn rose from the pillow. "Mom, where's Johnny? Is he here yet?"

"Yes, Gracie Lyn, he's here, but you must lie down—you're very sick."

Pulling at her sticky, damp nightgown, Gracie Lyn cried out, "Mommy, why am I in bed? Why am I all wet?"

"You've been sick, but you're better now. You're going to be okay," Edna whispered as she took the small, frightened child into her arms, frantically kissing her head, neck, and cheeks.

Hearing the rumbling of a car pulling into the driveway, Edna lay Gracie Lyn gently back on the pillow and stood up to see who was outside.

The tall, big-boned woman came bursting through the door, "Edna, what happened? Do you know what's wrong with Gracie Lyn?" the obviously worried woman exclaimed.

"Mom, it's alright now. She has malaria, but her fever just broke about an hour ago."

"Malaria!" exclaimed Gracie Lyn's Grandma Parsons.

"Yes, she had a 105-degree fever for five days. We couldn't get it to go down, so Doctor McAdams took a blood sample to Little Rock and had it tested. He gave her sulfa medicine, and she's better now. She'll be fine," Edna said.

"No one is fine after malaria, you wait and see—she will always be sickly," her mother announced

"Where is Uncle Johnny? Where is Uncle Johnny?" Gracie called out weakly.

The tall, lanky boy had patiently waited in the living room for hours. When he heard Gracie Lyn call his name, he came through the bedroom door. Glancing worriedly at Edna for approval, he slowly entered Gracie Lyn's bedroom. Edna gave him a nonverbal okay with a nod and a smile that said, "She's gonna be alright."

With his red hair tousled from constantly running his hands through the damp curls, and his freckled face flushed from the heat and worry, he approached his little niece.

With a wide smile, he said, "I'm here. I've been waiting for you to stop loafing around and get out of that bed so we could go riding."

Gracie Lyn smiled at her uncle. "I'm sick. Can you make me some chocolate milk?"

"Sure, and I'll make some toast with lots of butter, and show you how to dip your toast into the chocolate. We'll make chocolate toast," Johnny said with a grin.

Gracie Lyn gave him a wide smile. "Thank you, Uncle Johnny."

Chapter 11

Saturday, October 4, 1952
Miss Annie and Albert Meriwether's Farm

Just past sunrise, Gracie Lyn sat with her back against the old oak tree at the edge of the deep pool of crystal-clear water from an underground spring. This place of refuge wasn't protecting her from the outside world today. Her trembling hands were tight against her ears in an effort to block out the squeals of the young pig. She couldn't stand the sounds of the killing on slaughter day. Tears wet her face.

"God, why do you have people eat animals? Please, God, can't you change it? Can't we eat vegetables, eggs, and berries? I ain't gonna ever eat animals again. Please make it change," she pleaded.

The sounds of anguish coming from the barnyard stopped abruptly. Removing her hands from her ears, Gracie Lyn took a deep breath and let it out slowly. Exhausted from the trauma, she lay on the soft green moss that covered the ground at the base of the tree. The moss felt cool against her cheek. Turning over onto her back, she felt herself relax.

"Daddy's going to beat me again for running away, but this is where I belong," she said softly. "I wish I could stay here forever."

High above, orange and gold leaves rustled in rhythm with the October breeze, while a woodpecker pecked away at the trunk of the tree above her. The umbrella-like canopy provided adequate shade for the small child while the music of the enchanted woods lulled her into the beauty of sleep. On this beautiful day, the birds sang, the frogs croaked, and the cacada trilled to their friends. Edna called and called, but Gracie Lyn didn't hear her mother. Edna's voice was lost within the music of nature's symphony.

Gracie Lyn often visited the spring alone, waiting quietly for hours until the creatures of the woods came to drink from the cool clear water. She could sit without moving for such a long time that not even deer were afraid to come drink while she was there. Of all the thousand acres available to Gracie Lyn, this was her favorite place to spend her time. She thought that this beautiful place, with its spring, wildflowers, moss, trickling water, birds, and butterflies, must be a home for fairies. She went to the spring often and waited, but regretfully, a fairy never came out of hiding.

By late afternoon, the family had finished butchering the pig. The men had cut up, salted, and placed the meat in the smokehouse. In the yard, rendered pig fat sat in big covered black pots for soap-making on another day. The delicious smell of pork chops cooking on the big woodstove in the kitchen floated through the air, reminding the hardworking family why this job of butchering was so important. The hog they butchered today would sustain them through the winter and most of next year.

Gracie Lyn cautiously entered the little gate going into the backyard area of the old farmhouse. She quickly stopped in her tracks when she saw William resting on the back porch.

He called out to her, obviously angry, "I told you to stay here and help today. You were not to run off to the woods like that again."

"I cain't help it, Daddy. I cain't stand it, and I won't do it. You can spank me all you want. I cain't do it," Gracie Lyn cried as she turned toward the barnyard, where her grandmother was busy with the evening milking.

"You come back here, young lady. You are gonna get a whooping," he bellowed as he jumped from the porch.

Gracie Lyn heard a little pop sound come from her shoulder as William grabbed her arm and jerked her around. With the wide belt in his hand, he struck her repeatedly. Making only a whimpering sound every time the belt struck her frail legs, she never cried out. It seemed that the less sound she made, the harder he needed to hit her. Trickles of blood ran down her legs and onto her dirty bare feet.

Miss Annie running from the barn cried out, "William, leave her alone and let her be. Don't hit that child again. Don't hurt her again."

The short, stocky woman grabbed his arm, jerked the belt from his hand, and yelled, "William, I said you stop it right now, or I'll use this damn belt on you and make your legs bleed. You ain't gonna hurt that child ever again while I'm alive."

This was so unlike Miss Annie that both William and Gracie Lyn were startled in disbelief. Annie was the quiet, soft-spoken, loving woman who never raised her voice to anyone or anything. The anger in her voice validated the look in her eyes. Seeing this, William suddenly felt the shame of his actions and backed away from Gracie Lyn.

"You know her cain't be watching the butchering. Her is just a little girl," Miss Annie yelled at the man that towered over her.

"She cain't talk to me like that, Miss Annie—she has to know that," William said, almost cowardly.

"She's upset about the pig. It was her favorite of the litter. She bottle-fed the dang thing. You ain't going to beat this girl for loving that pig."

Gracie Lyn flung herself at her grandmother and grabbed her around the waist, "MaMaw, Stinky was my favorite. Daddy knew he was my favorite," she cried out, sobbing.

Trying to change the subject and distract the girl from the pain in her shoulder and cuts on her skinny legs, Miss Annie said warmly, "Come on, child—let's go clean you up and see what PaPaw is doing. I bet he'll agree to take you to town tomorrow to see the Halloween decorations in Jacksonville."

Chapter 12

Saturday, October 4, 1953
Kellogg Café, Garberville, Missouri

The two boys sat in the booth near the front door of the small cheerful restaurant. Hunched over his dish of ice cream and pie, Billy filled his mouth too full and mumbled, "I sure like lemon ice box pie."

"Me too—it's my favorite," Sam replied, wiping a tiny smear of lemon cream from his chin with a napkin.

"You are lucky with your pop havin' a restaurant. You can eat pie anytime you want."

"Yeah, I guess I am, but sometimes I don't think about it. What do you want to do after? Are you going someplace with Bobby today?"

"No!" Billy answered a bit too quickly and too loudly.

Sam looked up surprised. "I didn't mean anything by asking."

"I know. I'm just tired of Bobby trying to be my big brother all the time." Changing the subject quickly, Billy asked, "I told Jerri I would come over today—do you want to go with me?"

"Is she your girlfriend?" Sam asked with a little smirk.

"No, she's just a friend. She helps me with my homework. She's nice, and we have fun together."

"I'll go with you. I've been wantin' to see what's inside that big ol' house she lives in."

"It's her granny's house. Jerri's family has owned it for a really long time."

Later, under the shade of the huge willow tree, the three young people lounged on the grass of the sprawling lawn with Jerri between them. "Want to go to the carnival tonight?" she asked.

"Sure, I forgot about the carnival being in town," Billy answered. "Sam, you want to go?"

"Dang right. I hear they have a lady with a beard and a donkey-faced man at this thing."

Friday, May 16, 1955
Main Street, Garberville, Missouri

As Billy rapidly walked down the street, beads of sweat formed on his forehead and ran into his eyes. He pulled up the tail of his cotton shirt and removed the wetness. God, it's hot, but I don't want to go swimming today, he thought. Billy's plan to get home before Bobby found out that he wasn't waiting at the school like usual was all he could think about this afternoon. "Damn it, I don't care how much Bobby loves me. I never want to go swimming with him again. What am I going to do?" he said loudly. He started to pass Jerri's house but stopped, thought for a moment, turned around, and entered the long walkway to the beautiful house set back from the street.

"Jerri understands, and she's right. I was too young to know it was wrong. She said it's against the law. Maybe she can help me convince Bobby to stay away from me. Oh God! What if someone at school finds out? Oh shit! What if Sam finds out? He already thinks Bobby is strange."

He knocked at the door. The door opened, and in the doorway stood the plain girl with brown eyes so large and magnificent that you didn't notice that she might otherwise be considered less than beautiful. Even though Jerri was only sixteen, she had a look of someone much older and wiser.

"You look hot—come on in. It sure is hot for May. I'm making some ice tea—want some?" she offered as she stepped back and opened the door wider.

"Alright," Billy replied. He followed her into the kitchen and watched as she reached up and brought down two ice tea glasses from the kitchen cabinet.

"Let's go out and sit under the oak tree, and you can tell me why you look so upset," she offered.

"Alright," Billy replied again. Now, standing in her kitchen, he felt anxious and wasn't sure he wanted to talk about his problem. She had surprised him with her information, and now his involvement with Bobby seemed even worse than he first thought.

How does she know so much about it, and how does she know it's against the law? Will she tell the sheriff about Bobby and me? No, I know she won't tell. She's my best friend, he thought as he followed her to the backyard.

Billy and Jerri sat under the shade tree sipping cold ice tea, enjoying the serenity of the flower garden. Several minutes went by before Jerri asked, "Come on, Billy, what's up? Did you talk to Bobby?"

"Yes, and he was upset. He told me I couldn't stop going swimming with him," Billy answered.

"What? That creep! You can do anything you want. He has to leave you alone if you want him to. Remember, Billy, as I told you before—it's against the law. It's called child molesting for a man his age to mess around with a kid," she said angrily.

"I told him that, but he said I would get in trouble too. He said that it would be in the newspaper, and everyone would know what we did," Billy said, his voice quivering.

Jerri turned and looked him in the eyes. "You did nothing wrong. It was him. He is the adult, and you were just a little kid. You didn't know."

"He loves me," Billy said.

"Do you love him?"

"I don't know. He really seems to care about me and wants me to be with him. But I don't like it anymore. It feels wrong. I want it to stop."

There was silence for what seemed to be five minutes before Billy asked, "How do you know about all this stuff, Jerri?"

Her head jerked around. Staring into Billy's innocent face, her dark-brown eyes turned even darker. "I just know, that's all," she exclaimed with a don't-ever-ask-me-again look. They both became quiet again.

Billy stood and said, "I guess I'll go now."

At that moment, Jerri reached up and grabbed his arm, pulling him back into the chair.

"Wait, I have an idea. You must tell Bobby that you're going to tell Larry. Larry is his cousin, and if you say it like you mean it, Bobby will be afraid and stop being so pushy. If he doesn't stop, you may have to tell Larry. Larry will be very mad, and he'll tell Bobby to stop. He won't go to the police because Bobby is his cousin. Right?"

"Do you think so?" asked Billy, looking hopeful.

"Yes, yes, yes," she replied.

"That's a great idea, Jerri. I'm going to tell him that. He won't dare bother me anymore because I know he's afraid of Larry," Billy said as he jumped up and hurried toward the house. "I'll let you know what happens. See you tomorrow at school."

Monday, May 19, 1955

Billy didn't see Bobby's truck parked at the side of the house when he bounded up the steps onto the front porch and entered the living room.

"Hey there, Billy. I must have missed you after school Friday. I thought we were going swimming, it being so hot and all."

Billy walked past Bobby and into the kitchen. He could feel his face turning red, and his hands began to shake.

"I promised Jerri I would stop by her house after school," he called over his shoulder.

"Billy, Bobby is staying for dinner. Will you go to the garden and get me some tomatoes?" Nell called from the kitchen.

"Where's the bucket?" Billy asked quickly.

"I'll get it and help you," Bobby replied.

The tomatoes hung from the vine plump and inviting to anyone with a craving for something sweet and juicy on this hot afternoon. Billy reached down and picked a couple of tomatoes from a vine in the first row and silently stood there looking at the ripe fruit.

Suddenly, Bobby dropped the bucket, grabbed Billy by the shoulders, and turned him around so that they were now face-to-face. "You were not waiting for me after school Friday, and I don't like it. When I tell you we are going swimming, we are going swimming, you hear?" Bobby snarled.

Billy dropped the tomatoes and turned his face away from Bobby. Bobby's lips pressed together tightly, his forehead furrowed, and his eyes narrowed as he grabbed Billy's chin and turned his head around again.

Billy felt a terrible fear run through his young body. He had never seen Bobby so angry. As he looked back at him, he realized more than ever that it had to stop, and it had to stop now, no matter what happened in the future.

Standing straight up and puffing out is young chest, Billy announced, "Bobby, I told you I don't want to go swimming anymore, and if you don't leave me alone I'm going to tell Larry,"

"You wouldn't!" Bobby yelled.

"I would—you wait and see," Billy yelled back. "You know Larry would beat the shit out of you if I told him. I'm serious. I don't want to do it anymore, Bobby."

"You stupid little shit. You'll be sorry you said that," Bobby said as he stomped back toward the house.

Billy's knees were weak, and his hands trembled as he reached down, picked up the bucket, and left the sweet ripe tomatoes lying on the ground.

Chapter 13

Friday, December 16, 1955
Lawrence High School,
Lawrence, Missouri

When the buzzer blared ending the game, a roar of cheers filled the auditorium. The basketball court overflowed with students and players. A crowd gathered around Gracie Lyn, some hugging, some simply patting her on the back, giving accolades of "good job," "that's the way to go," or "that was amazing." She just stood there in shock. She couldn't believe that she really made the basket from that far away.

Because she was the new girl at this high school, Gracie Lyn was surprised when the coach picked her for the team. She was even more surprised that she did so well.

William had decided to move back to Missouri and rent a house in Lawrence instead of staying on the farm with Albert and Annie. Gracie Lyn hoped it would be a permanent move this time. She liked being on the team and having the opportunity to have friends living nearby.

Lawrence had a population of only about four hundred, but the school district included all the farm families for ten miles around. The campus for both the elementary and high school was quite large. Gracie Lyn had gone to school in Lawrence for part of the first grade, all of the second and third, and part of the fourth and fifth. Now, coming back for the ninth grade, she knew most of the students, and had renewed friendships with several girls in her class. Today she had become their hero, and this was the best surprise of all.

In the locker room, everyone talked about the fact that Lawrence had finally won a game against Garberville. Gracie Lyn sat quietly on the bench listening to the conversations.

Hurrying across the locker room, Coach James approached Gracie Lyn. His smile was so big that she could see his crooked teeth all the way to his molars. "Boy, Gracie Lyn, that was some game you played there."

Gracie Lyn smiled. "I didn't know I could do that."

"Well, young lady, I'm going to expect you to do it again when we play Jacksonport after Christmas. Do you think you can?"

"I don't know," Gracie Lyn replied.

Barbara Lynn, a star player on the team, approached Gracie Lyn. "Well, maybe it wasn't a mistake that the coach put a ninth-grader on our team," she snarled with her upper lip curled in a forced smile. "I guess you think you're a big shot now. Can you do that again? I bet not," she announced. Not waiting for a reply, she turned around and hurried away to join the celebration.

"Don't pay attention to her—she'll get over it," Coach assured Gracie Lyn.

Joella and Gloria came bounding into the locker room. "Gracie Lyn, Gracie Lyn, you were great. Come on, we're going to the Dairy Queen—come with us," Joella said excitedly, her golden curls bounced around her rosy cheeks as she jumped up and down, still excited by the outcome of the game.

"We're so happy you moved back to Lawrence," Gloria said.

Gracie Lyn felt a surge of emotion well up in her chest. Friends, she realized. Even if the other players don't like me, I do have friends here.

After dinner, Gracie Lyn screamed at her father, "But, Daddy, we can't go back to California again. I like it here. I'm on the basketball team. They're counting on me!"

Startled, he raised his hand to slap her, but stopped and brought it down to his side, then clenched it into a fist and yelled back, "Don't you ever talk to me with that tone of voice, young lady. I have a job in California. A good job! We are going!"

Taking a big breath to calm himself, he walked to the girl, placed his hand on the top of her head, and ruffled her hair. "You'll be okay, honey. I'm sorry about moving so many times last year."

She moved out of his reach. "I went to four different schools last year; I had no friends all year, and now I have friends. I don't want to go to California. What about Christmas with MaMaw and PaPaw? We have to have Christmas with MaMaw and PaPaw," she cried out hatefully as she walked toward her bedroom door.

Turning abruptly, with eyes wide open with hope, she asked, "Maybe I can stay on the farm with PaPaw and MaMaw? They love me; they will not want me to go."

"That's out of the question," William replied. "No more talk. Start packing—we're leaving tomorrow."

Stunned, she asked, "Tomorrow? What about school? Don't I need to tell them at school?"

"You'll only miss a week before Christmas vacation starts. Hush now, we'll handle that when we get to San Jose," he answered as he walked out the front door.

Tuesday, January 3, 1956

Gracie Lyn sat quietly in the chair while the school counselor filled out the paperwork for her classes.

This school looks brand-new. I wonder how long Dad will stay in San Jose this time before he wants to go back to Missouri. That's okay—they don't have a basketball team anyway, Gracie Lyn thought, looking around the office.

The smiling counselor handed Gracie Lyn a few papers and said, "We're a new school, only opened this year. We only have freshman and sophomore classes this year, but next year everyone here now will continue as juniors and seniors, and we will continue adding freshmen and sophomores. Here's a list of your classes, the room numbers, and your teachers' names. The school is small, so it won't take you long to find your way around."

Pointing out the window at the large building just opposite the parking lot, she said, "There's an assembly starting right now. Walk down to the gym and find a seat. You'll go to the third-period classroom afterward."

Entering the building, Gracie noticed an empty bleacher seat just inside the door near two girls. She sat down next to a pretty petite girl with long black hair.

The girl turned and looked her over, head to toe, and then said in a loud full voice, "Well, hi there, you must be new. Welcome to our assembly talk on the Devil Marijuana and heroin.

Gracie Lyn stared at her a minute before saying, "What?"

"You know—marijuana," the girl said again. Turning around in her seat to look directly at Gracie Lyn, she said, "You don't know about marijuana? Have you been hiding in a cave somewhere?"

Eyes wide with confusion, Gracie Lyn shook her head slowly back and forth.

"Well, you see, you smoke marijuana, and you give yourself an injection in the arm with heroin. It makes you feel good, like you're drunk or something like that. I do it all the time. You should see my arms," the girl said, laughing.

The principal walked up to a microphone and said to the assembly of students, "Quiet. Quiet please The film is about to start."

The lights dimmed and on the projector screen the words "The Devil Marijuana" appeared in large red letters.

When "The End" appeared on the screen, Gracie Lyn rose quickly and began examining the papers in her hands.

The petite girl stood next to her. "Can I help you find your class?"

Remembering what she said about using marijuana and heroin, Gracie Lyn walked away while saying quietly, "No, that's okay. I think I can find it."

The girl said in a laughing voice, "Hey, wait up. I was just kidding about using that stuff. I've never used it. Everyone here thinks the movies are funny, so we make jokes about them. Come on, let me help you."

Gracie stopped and looked down into the friendly face and smiled. "Okay, but that movie sure was somethin'. I never saw anything like that in Missouri."

The girl held out her hand. "Hi, I'm Rosie."

Gracie Lyn smiled. "I'm Gracie Lyn, but please just call me Gracie. I don't like Gracie Lyn."

As Rosie walked Gracie to the classroom, she said, "Missouri, huh? I like your accent. It's pretty cute. Hey, girl, there's a party this weekend at my friend's house, and you should come. You can meet some kids. My boyfriend is coming, and he has a friend I think you'll like. His name is J. T. Since you both are so tall and skinny, you'll be perfect for each other!"

Gracie looked at her. "Skinny?"

Rosie, laughing loudly, said, "Just kidding."

Chapter 14

Friday, May 16, 1958
Garberville High School,
Garberville, Missouri

Billy's feet and legs moved rhythmically to the three-quarter beat of the music, while his body twisted and turned smoothly with Sue Anne in his arms. He turned her away from his body with his left hand and with her right hand in his. Then he twirled her around and around until he reached for her and pulled her to him again.

"Wow." She smiled. "I didn't know I could do that."

He laughed quietly, his brown eyes bright in the pleasure of the moment. The music stopped, and they backed away from each other a little.

"You did that well," he remarked as they turned to go sit down.

Looking toward Billy, she said with a smile, "I had the best dancer in school leading me." The music started up again, this time a rocking beat of Maybelline.

"I love this song," she said as Billy took her hand and they moved onto the dance floor.

Again, feet moved rhythmically, but this time faster and with more purpose. Billy's hands pushed his partner away and quickly pulled her back again. Their young bodies twirled and twisted to the beat of the rhythm guitar in a flurry of fun. No one on this dance floor was thinking of school, homework, teachers, mothers, or fathers at this moment. It was all about dancing and feeling alive.

The next day Billy walked into the Marshall's Drug Store and Malt Shoppe, where he found Jerri already in a booth licking a double scoop of chocolate swirl ice cream in a sugar cone. His face full of joy and excitement, he said, "I had a great time last night," as he scooted into the seat opposite her.

"That's what senior balls are supposed to be like," Jerri said. "I had a great time last year too, although I did go alone. Was Betty Ann there?" she asked.

"No, should I feel bad?" Billy asked.

"You asked Sue first, and how were you to know that Betty Ann had such a big crush and wanted to claim you? Are you fixin' to ask Sue to the movies?"

"No, she's just a friend. I'm not going to ask Betty Ann either," Billy answered, dropping his head and looking down at the black-and-white tiled floor.

"Billy Baxter, you are one of the most handsome boys at Garberville High School. Of course, all the girls want you to be their boyfriend and go steady with you. The right girl will come along, and things will change for you. You don't have to feel bad about Betty Anne. She'll have a crush on someone else next week," Jerri reassured him.

"I'll take a Cherry Coke," Billy stated as the pretty waitress approached with a smile. "I don't know, Jerri—I'm confused. The other day Larry asked me if I had a girlfriend, and when I said no, he looked at me in a strange way. I changed the subject. I didn't want to start a conversation with him about why I haven't found a girlfriend. Mom never says anything about it. I don't worry too much about what she thinks. Most of the time she's too busy arguing with Larry to notice what I'm doing. I guess that's good, for me at least. Why cain't I just have lots girlfriends and let that be okay?"

Jerri laughed. "You do have a lot of girlfriends, and it is okay. They hang around you all the time, and like I said before, someday you will want to claim one of them "

"I know, I know." Billy laughed too. "I have fun with them, and I love to dance, but so far there's nobody I want to claim."

"Nothing wrong with that," Jerri reassured him again.

"What are you going to do after graduation?" Jerri asked.

"I have no idea. Maybe move to Little Rock and get a good job. You're lucky having your grandma's trust fund. You can go to college. If I don't get a job, Larry will want me to work with him. I'm no mechanic. I hate working on cars," Billy said.

Jerri jumped up from the seat and said, "Let's not worry about what's gonna happen tomorrow. Let's drive out to Hilltop and see who's hanging out there today. We'll forget about the future for now and just dance our butts off. "

Jerri's red sedan rumbled down the winding mountain road toward the Hilltop Dairy Queen just outside city limits. Turning into the graveled parking lot, she stepped hard on the brakes and came to a skidding stop, gravel flying everywhere.

"Whoa!" Billy exclaimed, hearing the loud thumping sound that came from the underside of the car as the gravel bounced off the carriage. They both started to laugh as they got out of the car and walked arm in arm to the outside covered dance floor and into the fun room at back of the hamburger joint.

The room, painted a bright blue, matched the red and blue juke box standing in the corner. Several teenagers were hanging out, playing cards, and dancing. Everyone knew one another, and most were good friends. In a small town, it was common for kids to meet in kindergarten and be friends throughout high school. Most stayed in the town, married someone from school, and the couples remained friends for the rest of their lives.

Billy strolled to the juke box, put a nickel in, selected "It's All in the Game," and pushed Play. He walked toward the door that lead to the outdoor dance floor, turned, and looked at Jerri. His brown eyes sparkled as he gave her a nod and a sexy sly grin in an unspoken suggestion to dance. She laughed loudly at this flirting joke and followed him out the door.

Saturday, May 17, 1958
William and Edna's house
Rhonda Drive
San Jose, California

The sky-blue two-door Ford Galaxy came to a screeching stop in front of the small yellow and white flattop house. A beep beep came from the car horn just as the front door opened and Gracie came running out with her cardigan sweater in one hand and her purse in the other. As she stood by the passenger side of the car, the thin young man reached across the seat and opened the door.

"Good thing Dad wasn't home to see you pull up and honk like that. You know he expects you to come to the door," Gracie said sweetly as she got in the car.

"I knew he wasn't home," J.T. replied. The car moved onto the street and quickly sped up.

"Where are we going?" Gracie asked, looking J.T. with the smiling blue eyes.

"We're going to my house. My mom and dad are gone for a few days. I thought we could fool around a little at the house. Judy is at our grandmother's, and Rebecca is in the city with her boyfriend."

Gracie's eyes widened as she turned to him. "I know what you want to do, and you know I'm not ready. My dad will kill me if I get pregnant. No that's wrong—he will kill you"

"We've been going steady for almost three years; do you think you will ever be ready?" J.T. asked, his eyes narrowing, his lips becoming a firm line across his thin face as he gripped the steering wheel tightly.

She turned sideways in the seat so she could look at his face, and said harshly, "I told you I would let you know when I'm ready, and I'm not ready now."

"Okay! Okay! We can just fool around at the house, but you promised you would think about it and tell me when you're ready, right?" he said. He turned his blond curly head toward her. With a mischievous smile on his rugged young face, he winked.

Suddenly Gracie clapped her hands together with excitement, "Oh, by the way the spring dance is in two weeks, and I want you to take me."

"Spring dance? Will they allow me on the campus since I quit school? Do you remember what the principal said about me hanging around the campus now that I don't go there anymore?"

"I know, but he can't keep me from having a date for the dance," she said, and then teasingly she asked, "I can't go to the dance alone, can I?"

J. T. frowned but said nothing as he turned the car onto a quiet street with large oak trees and finely trimmed lawns. He entered the driveway of a blue and white ranch-style house and stopped. As he turned off the car engine, he moved his body all the way around in his seat and looked at her with smoldering blue eyes and said, "Just depends. Let's go into the house and we'll talk about it."

As she opened the car door and hopped out, she giggled. "You'll take me to the dance. I know you will."

"I will if you give me what I want."

"Oh, J. T., you are such a bad boy,"

Later, Gracie entered the front door of her house and headed toward her room. Smelling something good cooking in the kitchen, she stopped at the doorway and looked in. As Edna stood over the stove, she picked up a piece of meat from the skillet and dropped it into the mouth of the very large dachshund standing at her feet.

"Hi, Mom," Gracie said, giving her a little wave of her hand.

"Hi, sweetheart. Your dad should be home soon, and we will have dinner," Edna answered, smiling.

"Okay, I'll be in my room. Just call me when it's ready." As she entered the room and closed the door, she heard the front door open and her dad come in. She picked up the phone to call her best friend, Rosie. She was excited to tell her that J. T. said he would take her to the dance.

Before she had time to dial the number, her mom called out, "Your dad's home and dinner is on the table."

"Can I call Rosie first?" she called to her mom.

"Please come now. Dinner will get cold if you don't," her mother said.

She put down the phone and hurried into the kitchen.

Gracie gave her dad a kiss on the cheek as she rounded the table to sit down. Edna placed the dinner plate with a pork chop, mashed potatoes, and peas in front of her. Gracie was very hungry. It had been a long day, and she hadn't eaten since the morning.

Ignoring the fact that his daughter was wolfing down her food, William announced proudly, "I have some good news. As soon as school is out, we're going to go to Missouri for the summer."

"What?" Gracie said as peas dropped out of her mouth and onto her plate.

"We're going to Missouri for the summer," William repeated, looking a little shocked.

"Noooooooooooooo," Gracie yelled, "I don't want to go to Missouri."

"I thought you would like that," William answered in a surprised voice.

"I want to spend the summer with J. T. and my friends. You're not going to do this to me again are you?" Gracie yelled as she jumped up from the table, went to her room, and slammed the door.

Flopping down onto her bed, tears streaming down her cheeks, she picked up the phone to call Rosie.

Chapter 15

Saturday, August 16, 1958
Nell and Larry Parker's Home,

Coming in the back door, Billy walked through the kitchen and went straight to the bathroom. Turning on the water full force, he leaned over and splashed the cold liquid on his face repeatedly.

It must be a hundred degrees today, he thought. I'd like to go to the river, but I can't seem to enjoy it once I'm there. What if I run into Bobby?

From the doorway came a masculine voice. "What are you doing?"

"I'm hot. I'm cooling off," Billy replied.

"Come in the living room when you're finished," Larry said.

Billy turned and took the towel from the rack and slowly dried his face and neck, noticing he had wet the front of his shirt in his process of cooling off. He shrugged, turned, and walked toward the living room. At the doorway, he came to an abrupt stop. He felt his face turn red as beads of sweat popped out on his forehead. He tried to slow his obvious labored breathing as the old uncomfortable feelings of awkwardness and memories engulfed his mind.

  There was Bobby sprawled lazily on the sofa, his long skinny legs draped over the arm and a sly grin on his face. "Hi there, Billy," he said grinning sickly.

  Billy nodded in recognition.

  "Bobby wants you to go to Little Rock with him to pick up a washing machine," Larry said.

  "When?" Billy asked.

  "Monday," replied Bobby.

  Billy gradually walked toward the front door. Just before he reached the door, he turned to Larry and said, "I promised Jerri's dad that I would help her paint her room and bathroom next week." Quickly adding, "I'll get paid," as he grasped for an excuse not to go with Bobby. "I've got to go to Marshall's now. I'm supposed to meet Jerri there this afternoon to talk about it," he said as he went out of the door.

  Purposely Billy stopped and stepped back into the doorway. He turned his head slowly toward Bobby, glared for a second, and then said flatly, "Sorry." He turned back around and walked across the porch and onto the sidewalk. His body trembled, and tears filled his eyes. The closer he got to Main Street and Marshall's, the faster he walked.

  When he entered the Marshall's Drug Store, Jerri noticed Billy's shaking hands as he slid into the malt shop booth. "What's wrong, Billy?" she asked.

  "Bobby was at the house today and wanted me to go to St. Louis with him to pick up a washing machine. It was just an excuse to get me alone," he answered, holding his hands in an effort to stop the shaking. As Billy tried explained how he felt, he became more and more anxious.

  Jerri placed her hands over his and held them tightly. "Billy, maybe you need to threaten him again?"

Saturday, August 16, 1958
Star Route, Missouri

Gracie raced the yellow Mercury coupe down the rough graveled road on her way back to Garberville after visiting the farm. Dust poured in as she frantically rolled up the window.

"Whew!" she said aloud, "gotta love these roads." She knew she was driving too fast, but besides the heat and dust, it soon would be dark, and the legend of Raw Head and Bloody Bones of Two Mile Creek kept running through her mind. Even now that she was older and understood that such things didn't exist, the thought of it still frightened her.

Passed down from generation to generation, the story of a man on a horse, carrying his head in his hand, frightened the children that grew up in the Soda Creek area. Even the adults would look over their shoulder when riding horseback or driving in the area to make sure Raw Head wasn't following. Some legends stayed with you always.

Gracie loved sitting on her grandpa's lap while he told her stories of the Soda Creek area and the legend of her great-great-grandfather James Todd. James Todd was a friend of Jim Bowie's and an icon in Missouri before it was a state and during the Civil War.

When she was fourteen, she discovered that James Todd had been a Confederate and had kept slaves on his plantation. This information made the stories of his conquest seem less impressive. No matter how many times she told herself it was just the era, she wished it wasn't true. She thought her family members must be ashamed too because they never talked about it. When Gracie asked her grandfather if it was true he said, "Well, we ain't proud of everything James Todd did." She wasn't sure if that answer included the fact that during his lifetime James Todd had five wives and twenty children.

Gracie, still thinking of her Grandpa Albert's stories and Grandma Annie's loving attention, finally reached the paved roads in Flat Rock. She rolled down the car window to let in some fresh air and impulsively yelled, "MaMaw and PaPaw, I love you so much." She had already decided that afternoon while sitting on the porch with her grandparents that she didn't want to go back to California. The only problem now was how to tell her dad.

She had spent almost two months in Missouri; most of that time was in Garberville with her mom and dad's friends, Earl and Lenora Hodge, and their daughters Sarah and Sue. William had a chance for a good-paying job in St. Louis, and Gracie talked her dad into letting her stay with the Hodges. They all had been friends for many years. During her stay in Garberville, she discovered that she like the town, and had already made some friends with a couple of boys that lived nearby. Also, she loved her grandparents and loved going to the farm. Her dad had bought a horse named Rex, and even though he was a little wild, Gracie already had him following her commands pretty well.

"Why go back?" she asked, talking to herself. "I'll miss Rosie, that's for sure, but I'm still mad at J. T. for cheating on me with that girl Charlene. I just can't forgive him. I really need a change. Yes! I want to go to school in Garberville now," Gracie stated, with conviction. Excited and happy, she couldn't wait to tell her mom and dad of her decision.

As William pulled the truck into the driveway of Earl and Lenora's modest home, Gracie pulled in right behind him. She stopped the car abruptly and jumped out shouting, "Mom, Dad, you're back!"

William and Edna got out of the truck and met their excited daughter.

"Mom, Dad, I'm so happy that you came back early. I want to ask you something very important. Come in the house, hurry! Hurry, please," Gracie said as she jumped up and down and pulled on her dad's arm.

"Hold on there, missy," William said while holding Gracie by the shoulders. "Is there something wrong?"

"No, no, Daddy. I just want to talk to you about staying in Garberville so I can finish the twelfth grade here. I don't want to go back to San Jose. Please, please, Daddy, let's stay in Garberville, please," Gracie said, clapping her hands together like a six-year-old begging for a new pony.

William said, "Calm down! We'll go into the house and discuss this quietly. Gracie Lyn, you know I have a big job in California. I have to go back."

"No, No, Daddy, you can get a job anyplace. I know you can. I heard you say that."

"Gracie Lyn, we can't stay in Garberville. That's all there is to it," William said again loudly.

Pulling William by the arm, Edna coaxed, "Let's go inside and talk about this calmly."

Chapter 16

Gracie and Billy

Wednesday, September 3, 1958
Garberville High School

Carol quickly approached Gracie as she walked out of
the American History class. "You're from California, right?"

Gracie nodded and said, "Yes, I am."

"I'm going to Marshall's Drug Store after school and
have a Cherry Coke. We could walk down there together if
you like. It's the place some of us hang out after school."

"Sure, where should I meet you?" Gracie said.

"In front of the school after seventh period," Carol
replied over her shoulder as she hurried down the hall to her
next class.

Gracie turned and watched the girl walk down the hall.
Wow, she thought, how nice of her. Gee, everyone here is so
nice and friendly. I don't know why coming from California
is so special. They act as if I know movie stars or something.

Gracie met Carol in front of the high school after
seventh period class as planned. As they walked down Main
Street, Gracie took special notice of the beautiful antebellum

homes with large lawns filled with huge oak trees while trying to answer Carol's barrage of questions.

"Why did you leave California?" she asked.

"We were going to spend the summer with my grandparents on the farm, but after we got here, my dad had a job offer in St. Louis that he couldn't pass up. I talked him into letting me stay with their friends, Tom and Lenora Holbrook. They have two daughters in high school. Do you know them—Sally and Sara?"

"Yes, I kind of know them, but they don't hang out at the Hilltop. That's where a lot us go to dance, talk, and, you know—just hang out," she said with a giggle. "You were going to be here only for the summer. What changed your mind?" Carol asked.

"I decided to stay because I like Garberville. Also it's nice to spend time on the farm with my grandparents."

"How could you decide so quickly?"

"I guess what really made up my mind was that I found out my boyfriend in California had cheated on me."

"How did you find that out?"

"My best friend found out from her boyfriend, and she wrote to me and told me."

"I bet that hurt your feelings."

"Sure it did," Gracie said, frowning.

Seeing the distress on Gracie's face, Carol changed the subject. "Were you born in California?"

"No, I was born here, out at our farm near Soda Creek. It's out past Sulphur Rock near Lawrence. I really love the farm and living with my grandparents, but I wanted to go to school in Garberville instead of Lawrence. Everyone is so friendly, and everything is so beautiful here."

"I bet you have a lot of friends in California."

"Yes, and I miss them too. My boyfriend was so upset when I told him I wasn't coming back that he joined the Army."

"Wow, how did that make you feel?"

"I was surprised, but I didn't care."

"How do you like our high school so far?"

"I really like it. It's so small. My high school had three thousand students. That's considered a small school by California standards. Also, I really like everyone I met this summer."

"Who did you meet?"

"I met Charles, Doug, Mike, Clarence, and . . . oh yeah, a guy named Richard."

Carol rolled her eyes and replied, "Oh, no wonder."

They entered the store and approached the row of booths in the soda shop at the back of the pharmacy.

"Hi Jerri. Hi Billy," Carol said.

Carol sat down first, and Gracie sat across from her.

"Billy, I've got to go. Bye, Carol. See you guys later," Jerri said as she picked up her purse and scooted out of the booth.

"Okay, I'll see you later," Billy answered.

Turning around in his seat and leaning over the back of the booth, Billy said, smiling, "What'cha doing, Carol?"

"We're just talking. You want to join us?"

With that, Billy scooted out of the seat and slipped into the booth next to Carol facing Gracie.

"Gracie, this is my brother Billy. Billy, this is Gracie," Carol said.

With warm smiling eyes looking directly at Gracie, Billy said, "You must be the new girl from California I've been hearing about."

Chapter 17

Sunday, September 21, 1958
Miss Annie and Albert's Farm

Miss Annie set the fried chicken on the dining room table next to the mashed potatoes and gravy just as William and Edna pulled into the parking area by the house. Quickly she returned to the kitchen and called out the back door, "Albert, William and Edna are here. Bring in some fresh water from the well so I can make some sweet tea."

As William and Edna came in the front door, Miss Annie called out, "Y'all go sit down. I'm making tea. Albert will be there in a minute."

"Where is Gracie Lyn?" asked Albert as they pulled out their chairs to sit down for dinner.

"She went to the movies with a boy from Garberville. He seems like a nice boy, quiet and polite. I think he likes Gracie," Edna answered.

"At least he finished high school, not like J. T. He quit at sixteen," William added, obviously not happy with Gracie's old boyfriend.

Throughout the meal the discussion continued about Gracie and her decision to stay in Garberville. All agreed that staying in Missouri and having new friends seemed to be the thing for her.

Miss Annie looked hard at William and asked, "What do you think of Edna getting an apartment and staying with Gracie while you work in Illinois?"

"I think it's the only way we can let Gracie finish school in Garberville. Since I gave Gracie permission to go to the Hilltop Dairy Queen joint, where the most kids hang out, Tom and Lenora are not happy about having our freewheeling daughter living in their home, influencing their girls. Edna will stay in the apartment with Gracie, and I'll come back every other weekend."

Everyone except William had the same thought: "God, I hope William won't do something stupid while he is away."

Sunday, September 21, 1958
Shelba Movie Theater, Garberville

Gracie glanced in the direction of the boy sitting next to her in the dark theater and thought about how nice it felt when he took her hand and held it gently.

I'm surprise he hasn't tried to kiss me or get fresh, she thought. Gosh, I never got to see the whole movie when I was with J. T. He couldn't keep his hands off me. Billy is different. I like it. I think I'll ask him if he'll go to the farm with me next weekend. I wonder if he likes to ride horses.

Saturday, October 4, 1958
Miss Annie and Albert Meriwether's Farm

With the bridle in his hand, Billy slowly approached the big black horse. "Come on, boy—let me put this bridle on you so we can go for a ride," he said warmly.

Rex took a few steps forward, snorted, and gave Billy a look as if to say, "Forget it, you're not going to ride me." Billy moved near the horse. Rex's tail flew up and swished back and forth, warning him not to come any closer.

Billy threw bridle to the ground "Dang you, horse!"

"Haven't you caught that horse yet?" Gracie said mockingly as she came through the corral gate.

"Heck no, he's too wild. How do you ever get a bridle on him?"

"Like this," Gracie said as she walked up to the horse holding a handful of corn. As Rex reached for the corn, Gracie grabbed him by the mane and instructed, "Now, when I give him the corn, you come on up slowly and put the bridle on him just as he finishes."

Billy followed her orders, and the bridle went on smoothly. Gracie reached for the saddle hanging on the fence, and in a quick swoop, she turned and threw it onto Rex's back.

"Dang, girl, you know how to handle this horse," Billy said, smiling as the skinny girl tightened the buckles of the small English saddle.

"I've been riding since I was five—I should know something," Gracie answered, grinning. "We both can't ride in this small saddle, so you sit on the seat and I'll ride on the rump. I'll have to hang on to you, but we'll take turns. My turn is when we're on our way home," Gracie stated with authority.

Rex walked through the pasture with a slow diligence. Billy slapped his sides gently with a willow switch, but the horse wouldn't go any faster.

"Won't this horse trot?" Billy asked.

Gracie laughed. "Not when we're leaving the barn, but wait till we start back. You'll have to hang on tight then."

The crisp October air felt refreshing after the long, hot summer of 1958. The young couple engaged in small talk as they sauntered through the pasture and into the woods.

After a while Billy asked, "How much further?"

"Why?" Gracie asked. "Your butt starting to hurt?" She giggled.

"No!" Billy said defensively. "I was just asking."

"Not much further—just over that rise," Gracie said as they came out of the woods and entered another pasture.

"How many acres do your dad and grandfather own?"

"I don't know—two thousand I think," Gracie answered nonchalantly.

Surprised, Billy said, "That's a lot."

"See there, that big pond by that old house? We can stop there. MaMaw caught a five-pound bluegill out of that pond a few years ago. Once MaMaw and I stayed at the pond too late and had to walk down the road to get home instead of crossing the fields. We were almost home when a mountain lion crossed the road in front of us. He stopped in the middle of the road and stared at us for a little while, and then just went on across the road and into the field. Boy, we were scared, but he left us alone."

When they arrived at the pond, they dismounted. Gracie removed the quilt from Rex's back and spread it on a flat spot near the pond.

"Come, let's rest here," she said to Billy.

The soft, thick pasture grass was comforting as they lay on their backs looking up at the billowing clouds forming in the north. "Looks like we might be gettin' some rain," Billy said, breaking the spell of the quiet moments.

"Yes, guess we should head back pretty soon," Gracie answered sadly.

Billy turned his head toward Gracie and watched her profile for a few moments. He looked down at her hand placed comfortably at her side. Slowly and gently he slipped her hand into his and brought it up to his mouth and kissed her fingertips. She turned toward him and smiled sweetly. They lay peacefully until a drop of rain hit Gracie on the cheek.

"Oh, it's starting to rain—we'd better head back before the lightnin' starts."

Kaboom . . . rumble . . . rumble . . . The far-off sound of thunder was now overhead.

"Too late—we're in for rain," Gracie said loudly, jumping up from the blanket.

As they came in view of the barn, the lightning crackled above them, and within seconds the thunder clapped so loud Rex reared his head up in protest of the noise.

"Hang on," Gracie yelled as Rex galloped through the pouring rain with Billy bouncing roughly on his behind.

"I don't have a choice." Billy wrapped his arms tightly around her waist.

As they reached the gate to the corral, Gracie yelled, "Jump off and open the gate. Close it and make sure it's locked."

Once inside the corral, Gracie rode Rex into the stable and dismounted. Patting the exhausted horse, she led him to his stall. "Good boy, good boy," she uttered repeatedly.

"You were right. That horse sure can run when he's headed back to the barn," a rain-soaked Billy said as he walked into the stable.

After the downpour passed, the two teenagers ran across the road and into the farmhouse, where Miss Annie had supper waiting. Billy sat down and looked around the table at Gracie's family: the old grandpa Albert, the young grandma Miss Annie, Edna, Gracie, and William. Nice family, he thought, but Gracie's dad makes me a little uncomfortable.

When William started joking about Rex, and how hard Billy tried to catch the crazy horse, he felt even more comfortable at this table. Billy knew that William was a tough man, the kind of man that would only joke with someone he liked. He liked it here. He liked Gracie.

After supper, Billy stood up from the table and asked, "Which way to the bathroom?"

William laughed. "The outhouse is out the back door, through the gate, and down the path next to the fence. Since it's raining, you could slip behind the smokehouse if you want."

Billy's face turned red, and everyone at the table chuckled.

Chapter 18

Saturday, November 15, 1958
Marshall's Drug and Soda Shop

"Are you going to escort me to the Thanksgiving dance?" Gracie asked with a knowing smile

"Of course—we're going steady, aren't we?" Billy smiled back. "I'm very proud that you're one of the Thanksgiving Maids. I wonder if the football team would have voted for you if they'd known that we're going steady."

"I don't know, but I was surprised when the principal led me into his office and told me that they voted for me to be Homecoming Queen. When the principal ask me to step down, I didn't hesitate to say yes. I knew that senior-class girls would feel bad if someone became queen after only being at the school two months. I was afraid that if I was queen not one girl in the senior class would be my friend."

"I wonder what the football team thinks about what Mr. Hutchinson did."

"I don't know, but Coach Blair was supposed to explain it to them."

Billy gave her a hug, "We'll go to the dance, and you'll dance only with me. You'll be my queen."

Saturday, December 20, 1958
Jerri's home, Main Street, Garberville, Mo

Billy and Jerri came in the front door making shivering sounds and rubbing their hands together as they headed straight for the big rock fireplace at the back of the living room. "It must be thirty degrees out there," Billy said through chattering teeth.

"We need some hot chocolate to warm us up. I'll go to the kitchen and make it, and you can tell me what you wanted to talk about when I get back." Soon Jerri returned with hot chocolate and cookies. Setting them down on the table near the sofa, she said, "Come on over here and sit down and tell me what's going on with you these days. We haven't talked in a while."

Billy sat, and Jerri handed him a cup of chocolate. As he sipped, the warm liquid soothed his body and he relaxed.

"Are you and Gracie still together?" Jerri asked.

"Oh yes, we are, and it's good. She's very easygoing and kind of crazy sometimes, but a good crazy. You know what I mean?"

"Yes, I do know what you mean—fun kind of crazy."

Billy became serious and said, "Bobby came to my house when Mom and Dad were gone. He cried and said he missed me. He wants me to be friends with him again. He said there would be no hanky-panky, but I don't believe him."

"Do you still want to be friends with him?"

"Well, in some ways I've always missed him, and I know he loves me, but I don't think he really wants to just be friends."

Jerri scooted over close to Billy, took his face in her hands, and asked, "Billy, do you love Bobby, and do you want to be with him again?"

"No, no I don't."

"Are you sure?"

With tears in his eyes, he turned away from her, got up from the sofa, and walked to the fireplace. He stuck out his hands toward the flames as if to warm them. He turned and looked at her again. "I don't want that, Jerri. Honest, I don't want that. Besides, he's married now. Why is he asking me?" He turned back toward the fireplace and placed his hands over his face to cover the tears.

Jerri leaned over and put her arm around his shoulder. "It's okay Billy. It's okay."

Sunday, March 29, 1959
Gracie and Edna's Apartment,

On the deck, Gracie began to sniffle as Billy pulled her to his chest and wrapped his arms around her. "I'm going to miss you a lot while you're gone," she whimpered.

"I'll miss you too, but William is going to teach me to do drywall, and we'll only be gone a month. Besides, I didn't know how to say no to your dad when I don't have any job prospects here in Garberville."

"I know, but I'm still sorry you have to go to Illinois to work and I can't go."

Billy backed away from Gracie and said, "I promise I'll write to you every day if you'll promise to be good while I'm gone."

Gracie pulled back from his chest. "Of course I will. What do you mean, 'be good'? Do you mean going out with someone else? We're going steady. I'm not going out with anyone else," she answered quickly.

"Gracie, you know as soon as I'm gone other guys are going to ask you out. I know they will."

Gracie reached for Billy's shirt and pulled him close to her. "I don't want to go out with anyone but you, ever! Do you understand? Like the song: 'You are my guy, my guy, my guy'!" she said musically.

Laughing, Billy said, "Come on, you crazy girl—go ask your mom for the car keys, and let's go make out somewhere in the bushes before I have to go home. I'm supposed to meet your dad at five a.m."

"I already have the keys. You see—I planned ahead," Gracie said as she jingled the keys above her head.

Chapter 19

Friday, July 3, 1959
Nell and Larry Parkers' Home

Billy walked out the front door and stopped abruptly when he saw the blue Ford truck sitting at the curb. "Hey, Billy," Bobby yelled from the window.

"Hey, Bobby," Billy called back.

"Come in the truck so I can talk to you."

"No, Bobby, there is no need."

"Please Billy. I really want to talk to you."

Billy reached the truck and smiled at Bobby. "Okay, but I've got to meet Gracie at Marshall's in a few minutes." He walked around to the other side and opened the door. "Bobby, I can't go anyplace with you," he said as he slid onto the seat.

"Sure, kid. I'll give you a ride downtown, but first I want to talk."

Two hours later Billy walked into Marshall's, but as he expected, Gracie wasn't there. He walked up Main Street toward her apartment. He felt so ashamed. "What can I say to Gracie about not showing up? I can tell her I was with Bobby. She doesn't know anything—only that he's my uncle.

I'll tell her that I had to help him with hauling some hay and there wasn't time to stop by Marshall's. What am I going to do about Bobby? Damn, I don't know what to do now."

Saturday, July 4, 1959
River Park, Garberville

The red, white, and blue fireworks burst into the sky over the river, sending reflecting light over the smooth surface. The reverberating kaboom came seconds later. Gracie let out a deep loud "Oooooh" and "Ahhhh!" at every blast of sparkling light. Billy didn't seem to notice. Realizing that his attention wasn't on the fireworks, Gracie asked, "Billy, don't you like fireworks?"

"They're okay."

"What's wrong? You seem quiet tonight."

"I need to talk to you about something."

"What?"

"Not now. I want to go someplace private."

"Okay, let's go. It's no fun looking at fireworks if you are going to be a sourpuss." Gracie gave him a pout, trying to lighten the mood.

Billy drove the Mercury sedan slowly down the dirt road and into the trees. He parked just beyond the parking area where teenagers went to be alone. No one was there tonight. They were all at the Fourth of July celebration at River Park.

Billy cut off the engine and turned toward Gracie. Saying nothing, he sat and stared at her.

"Billy, what is it? You are scaring me," Gracie asked.

"I want to go all the way with you," he said flatly.

"What? Now? You mean now?"

"Now or later, I don't care. I just though you should know," he said flatly again.

"Have you gone all the way before?" Gracie asked cautiously.

"No, I've never wanted to before," he answered in a low, almost inaudible voice.

"Have you?" Billy asked.

"No, not really," Gracie answered softly.

"What do you mean, 'not really'?"

"Well, you know I had a boyfriend in California, and we made out a lot, but we never went all the way."

"Honest?" Billy asked.

"Honest," Gracie answered cautiously.

Friday, July 10, 1959
Hilltop Dairy Queen
City Highway, Garberville

Gracie slowly entered the Hilltop parking lot and pulled her car next to the dance patio. When she saw Billy standing with a group near the game room door, she called out, "Billy, can I talk to you?"

He walked to the car, went around to the passenger side, and got in without saying a word.

Gracie pulled the car to the end of the parking lot and stopped. With unwanted tears wetting her cheeks, she turned all the way around in the seat and asked, "What's wrong, Billy? I haven't seen you since . . . since . . . since that night. Now that we did it, you won't talk to me. I don't understand. Please tell me why."

Billy looked straight ahead, and in a low mean voice he said, "You lied to me—you weren't a virgin."

"What?" Gracie said, startled by his accusation. "Yes, I was! I never went all the way with J. T.!"

"You must have been with someone when I was working in Illinois with your dad."

"No I wasn't, honest." Gracie covered her face with her hands as hot tears filled her eyes and rolled down her cheeks.

"I think we should break up because I don't believe you," Billy said without a hint of emotion. He opened the car door and got out.

"Wait! Billy, I'm telling the truth!" she cried. He closed the door, walked around the car, and headed toward the patio. He never looked at her.

Saturday, August 15, 1959
Gracie and Edna's Apartment

Billy sat for four hours at the bottom of the long set of stairs that went up to Gracie's apartment before he heard the car pull into the driveway. He jumped when the porch light came on. Looking around the yard, he realized for the first time that it was late and dark. He looked down at his shaking hands. "Damn!" he said as he stood and placed them in his pants pockets. Hoping to calm his nerves, he took three deep breaths in a row.

"Thanks for taking me to the quarry. Maybe next time I'll be brave enough to go swimming; I'll talk to you tomorrow," Gracie yelled as the girl backed her car out of the driveway. With a large bath towel draped over her shoulder, and a flashlight in her hand, she jumped as she came around the corner of the walkway and found Billy standing there.

"What are you doing here?" she asked, obviously startled.

"I've been waiting all night to see you—please talk to me."

"Yeah, like you talked to me?"

"Please, Gracie."

"Billy, it's been weeks, and now you come here like I'm supposed to just forget what you said to me?"

"No, I don't expect you to forget. I talked to someone about that, and they said there are many different ways for a girl to lose her virginity."

"What? Just leave. I don't want to talk to you. By the way, I was a virgin until you got your bright idea!"

As she started to climb the stairs, Billy grabbed her hand; "No, wait, I love you so much, and I miss you. I'm sorry Please, Gracie, let me prove it to you."

Gracie looked into his pleading eyes, let out a frustrated sigh, and went to him, "Oh, Billy, I missed you too."

He wrapped her up in his arms and smothered his face in her long brown hair. They stood in the dark cool night clinging to each other, not saying a word. Billy pulled away first and suggested they sit and talk.

Sitting on the stairway step, Gracie said, "I don't want to talk anymore, Billy. I just want this to be over and the pain to go away,"

"Okay, but please believe me when I say I'm sorry."

They sat quietly on the bottom step holding each other, saying nothing, unaware of time, enjoying the peaceful feeling of being together.

Edna called from the apartment door, "Gracie, I see that you're out there with Billy, but you must come in now. It's midnight, and your dad will be home from Memphis early in the morning. We're going to meet him at the farm."

Chapter 20

Saturday, November 14, 1959
Center Theater, Garberville

Coming out of the movie theater, Gracie's full skirt billowed out as she twirled around. Clapping her hands, she said joyfully, "I just loved that movie."

Billy smiled and drew her to him. "Yes, I liked it too. It's kinda like us, don't you think?"

"Yes, yes, it's just like us. They were so in love," she said, snuggling into his side as they walked up Main Street towards Marshall's to have a hot chocolate before going home.

Billy suddenly stopped. Staring ahead, his arms tightened around her, "See that man coming down the street just ahead? See the tall man with the dark hair on the other side of the street?"

"Yes."

"That's my real father."

"What?" Gracie replied as she watched the tall man quickly cross the street with his head down, obviously avoiding the two young people.

"Hurry, let's go into Marshall's; I'll tell you about him inside."

Gracie scooted far into the booth, leaving room for Billy. To her surprise he sat on the other side facing her. She frowned when she noticed the sad look on Billy's face. Not knowing what to say, she stayed silent, waiting for him to talk. They ordered, but neither spoke until the waitress brought the steaming cups of chocolate with a mound of whipped cream and set them in front of them. Billy picked up a cup of chocolate and turned it around and around in his hands as he told Gracie about his real father.

"My mother was fifteen when I was born. That man is my real father. He has never spoken a word to me. He refuses to accept me as his son. Mom married Larry a few years later," Billy said.

Gracie stared at Billy in disbelief. All she could manage to say was "Really?"

"Seeing him tonight is ironic because last week I told Mom and Larry that I wanted to be adopted. I told them that I'm mad that they never thought of doing it before this. Mom said it was her fault. Larry wanted to adopt me, but she was the one that she didn't let it happen. I always thought it was because Larry didn't love me. Mom couldn't tell me why she didn't have Larry adopt me. I let them know that I need to have Parker be my legal name in case I wanted to get married. They agreed and promised to take care of it right away. Now you know I am not a Parker. I'm a bastard."

Gracie got up from her side of the booth and scooted into the seat beside Billy. "I don't know what to say except don't be sad—your real dad is a jerk and doesn't deserve you as a son. I love you, and since I don't know what a bastard is, and as long as I can't catch it, I don't care."

Laughing, he wrapped his arms around her and squeezed her so tight she had a hard time breathing. Gracie sat there and let him squeeze until she finally gasped for breath.

Billy pulled away. "I'm sorry—I got carried away. It felt good."

"I'm so sorry, Billy. I had no idea that Larry wasn't your dad."

"Let's forget about it for tonight and go to Hilltop. I think they have my favorite song on the jukebox now."

"Which song?" Gracie asked.

"'Smoke Gets In Your Eyes.'" Billy smiled as he gave her a little push with his body indicating they were leaving the booth. "Tomorrow we can go to the farm and ride Rex out to the pond. I'll tell you more of my family secrets if you tell me yours."

"I promise," Gracie said.

Looking down, he hesitated for a moment and said, "I love you."

Chapter 21

Wednesday, December 30, 1959
Gracie and Edna's Apartment

"Billy Scott, I can't take this anymore. You've got to stop doing this and trust me. You don't trust me, and it's driving me crazy. You hound me when you're home, and when you're away your letters accuse me of cheating. You say mean things to me, and it hurts," Gracie cried.

"How can I trust you? You stay out all night and don't tell me."

"I didn't know you were coming home. I was with my friends. We hung out at the quarry, and driving home we found an old pumpkin patch and took some pumpkins left behind from the picking. We always do stupid stuff like that. It's fun just to hang out all night together. And besides, that's only the second time."

"But Charlie and Rick were with you," Billy said angrily.

"Yes, and so were Lucie, Emilee, and Marie. No one was with anybody. We are just friends. The worst thing we did was follow Evan in his milk truck and took bottles of milk from people's porches and put about ten bottles of milk on Dick's porch. We thought it would be funny when he went out to get the milk in the morning. At five, we went to the Blue Bonnet bakery, and Steve gave us two loaves of fresh hot baked bread. We did nothing more than that," Gracie screamed in frustration.

Billy ran his hand through his hair and let out a big sigh. "I'm at work for two weeks at a time, and all you do is play around."

"That's not true. I'm going to beauty school almost every day," Gracie rebutted.

"Almost every day?" Billy asked, raising an eyebrow. "You should be almost finished by now, and you still have three months to go. Your dad told me that. He's not happy with what you're doing either."

"I'm seventeen, and I want to have fun. I'm not doing anything wrong. My friends are home for Christmas vacation, and we are just hanging out. I'm having fun." Turning her back to Billy, Gracie said quietly, "Maybe we should break up since I'm causing you so much worry?"

"Maybe we should," Billy said as he turned and walked away.

Saturday, February 13, 1960
Garberville Beauty College

With the mirror in her right hand, the tiny elderly woman turned the swivel chair around and checked the back of her head. Admiring the perfect finger waves in her salt-and-pepper gray hair, she said, "Gracie Lyn, my hair looks beautiful. You're a good little beauty operator."

"Thank you, Miss Safford. I appreciate that."

Gracie finished putting her combs and clips in the drawer just as Lavern approached and asked, "Gracie, are you going to be here tomorrow? I saw a new set and haircut at the conference in St. Louis, and I want the students to learn how to do it. It's called the Bubble. Everyone in the big cities is wearing it. It's not hard to do, but there is a lot of back-combing."

"Sure, that sounds like fun," Gracie said happily. "Miss Lavern, may I leave early today? It's Valentine's Day, and I have a date."

"You still goin' with that Mitchell boy over in South Side?"

"Yes. Why?"

"I saw you two at the Dairy Queen, and he looked like he's in love."

"He's nice, but it's not serious."

The big redhead tenderly put her arm around Gracie's shoulder, "Don't worry, honey. You'll leave this town someday and go to some big city, buy your own beauty shop, and be a big success. Billy Parker will just be a teenage memory."

"You really think that, Miss Lavern?"

"Sure do, kid."

Chapter 22

Thursday, March 24, 1960
Hilltop Dairy Queen

Johnny Ray placed the closed sign in the window, turned off the Hilltop's "Hamburger and Shakes" sign, slipped off his dirty apron, opened the cash register, and removed a few bills. As he walked out the back door he called out to the young people hanging around his car, "Any of you that are going with me to Cave City, go ahead and get in the car. I'll be there in a minute. I'm going to check the back room."

When he opened the door, Gracie and Jinny Anne were playing cards at the corner table.

"I'm closing up and going to Cave City for some supplies. A few people are going with me. Do you two want to go and keep me company?"

Gracie said, "I'll go."

"I can't. Mom is expecting me home for dinner," Jinny Anne said.

Gracie saw several people crawling into the station wagon, and as she walked closer she said, "I think this car is full."

Someone from the shadows of the backseat encouraged, "I'm sure there's room for one more in the backseat. Squeeze in."

"Okay," she said reluctantly. She opened the car door and started to scoot into the seat, when she heard a familiar voice.

"Hi there," Billy said, smiling.

Trying hard to keep her composure, Gracie answered, "Hi."

After several minutes of being ignored, Billy turned to her. "I haven't seen you in three months. What have you been doing?"

Gracie turned her head, looked at him, and smiled. "Just going to beauty school. I only have fifty-six more hours and I'll be finished. I bet you thought I wouldn't finish," she said jokingly.

"You're right. I didn't believe that you would finish. It's good to see you. I've missed you," Billy said sincerely.

Gracie's heart began to pound. "It's good to see you too."

"Mom and Larry are moving to Redlands, California, on Saturday," Billy said.

"Really? What are you going to do?"

"I'm going with them. I need to get out of Missouri," Billy said flatly.

"Oh!" Gracie said.

Picking up her hand, he said in a low voice, "Why don't you go with me?"

"Oh! Sure. Dad would kill me. The only way he would let me go to California with you is if we were married." Gracie laughed.

"So let's get married," Billy said as he kissed her hand.

Stunned, Gracie said, "I was joking."

Bill gave her a serious look. "I'm not joking. I love you."

"Billy, I love you too, but we can't get married in two days."

His large brown eyes looked at her pleadingly. "We can try."

Huddled in the backseat, Gracie and Billy discussed their options.

"How can we get married in two days?" Gracie asked.

"First we must talk to Larry. He knows a judge and the people at the clinic. Maybe he can get the permission to get the blood test today and waive the three-day wait," Billy said.

"Dad comes home from Illinois tonight. We'll have to tell him. Oh my gosh, I hope he won't try to stop us." Gracie's voice quivered at the thought of William and his usual reaction to things he didn't like.

"We will make this happen, Gracie," Billy said, pulling her closer.

Later that evening,

Gracie and Billy held hands as they slowly climbed the stairs to Gracie's apartment. Standing at the door, they looked at each other and kissed lightly before going in. Edna and William sat together on the sofa. Gracie sat on the chair next to her parents. Billy sat on the floor at her feet.

"Mom, Dad, this will come as a surprise, but Billy and I are getting married tomorrow at one o'clock. We're going across the street to Reverend Sommer's house. It's all been arranged. In the morning I'm going to Barnett's Department Store for a dress, Jinny Anne will go get me a bouquet at Smith's flower shop, and Billy is going to the jewelry store for gold wedding bands. We had our blood test this afternoon, and Larry got Judge Barnett to waive the three-day wait."

Shocked, Edna gasped. She looked first at Billy and then at Gracie. She reached for a tissue in her pocket and wiped the tears that filled her sad eyes. "I thought you two broke up."

"Mom, we got together this afternoon and discovered we can't live without each other," Gracie said.

Obviously shocked, William sat quietly at first. Trying hard to stay calm and not overreact, he said, "Are you sure you want to do it this fast? Why don't you wait and have a real wedding?"

Gracie reached over and took William's hand. "Dad, we love each other, and we're leaving for California on Saturday with Nell and Larry."

For an hour or more, Billy and Gracie discussed everything that had happened up to this point. They talked about how they would live once they arrived in California. They tried to convince the worried parents that they knew what they were doing.

William said nothing more. Sadly, he realized that because of their difficulties in the past, he couldn't fight his determined daughter this time. He saw too much of himself in her impulsive decision. To keep from showing his pain he stood and said, "I need to go to the farm. I'll be back in the morning. Edna, are you going with me?"

"No, I'll stay here with Gracie tonight," she said.

As William got to the door, he turned and asked Billy, "Are you sure, Billy? This is a big responsibility."

Billy hesitated a moment. "Yes, William, I'm sure."

Gracie came down the apartment stairs with a blanket in her arms. When she sat down, she wrapped the blanket around Billy, and the excess around her body. She snuggled close to him and asked, "How do you feel?"

"I'm okay, but are you sure we're doing the right thing? We could wait, and I could go to California on Saturday and send for you after I get a job."

Gracie didn't say anything. Minutes went by.

"What are you thinking?" Billy asked.

She burst into tears. "I'm thinking you'll go to California, get a job, meet new people, and then decide you don't want to marry me after all because you've convinced yourself that I've been unfaithful. Soon you'll forget about me because I'm far away. I don't think you love me at—"

Billy stopped her rambling words with a hard smothering kiss.

When he finally pulled away, he said, "Oh, honey. Forget what I said—we'll get married tomorrow just as we planned."

Chapter 23

Friday, March 25, 1960
Gracie and Edna's Apartment

Gracie sat quietly in a midcalf white cotton dress, while Billy nervously fiddled with two small gold bands in his sport jacket pocket. They sat in Edna's apartment waiting for William to arrive. Gracie watched her mom nervously twist a hanky while asking Billy more questions about the trip to California. Her black eyes showing a bit of pink at the rim from what Gracie was sure were from tears shed during the night.

"Mom, don't worry. I'm so happy, and we'll be just fine in California. If we don't like it in Redlands, we can go to San Jose. Look at all the family we have there. And besides, you and Daddy are supposed to come to California next year when that new job starts."

Edna looked up with a smile. "Gracie, you must know I'll miss you and, yes, I'll worry."

Billy spoke up. "It's almost one; we should go downstairs now."

"Where's Daddy? Don't tell me he's not coming. Mom, did he say he wasn't going to come?"

"No, but I'm not surprised. He said to me that he wasn't sure he could watch you get married."

"Okay, if that's the way he feels. He didn't make it to my graduation. What made me think he would be here for my wedding?"

"Don't be so hard on him, Gracie. This is very difficult for him. He loves you very much."

Gracie took a deep breath, smiled at her mother, grabbed Billy's hand, and said, "Oh, I know, I know. Come on, Billy—let's get married."

"Oh my goodness," Gracie squealed in delight as she reached the bottom of the stairs. Standing there on the walkway were a dozen of their friends. "Emilee, how did you do this?" Gracie asked in a higher-than-usual tone of excitement.

"Last night I called as many people as I could and told them to call the others. I went to the high school and asked Mr. Sanders to let Carol, Lucie, Robert, and the others out of class. They should be here any minute," Emilee Ann said.

Holding hands, Gracie and Billy entered the home of the retired pastor. The beautiful and inviting living room was a perfect setting for this wedding: a warm fire in the fireplace, lace curtains on the windows, the sun shining brightly into the room, and, best of all, the dignified elderly pastor waiting patiently at the back of the room ready to unite the young couple. Retired Pastor Sommer, Bible in hand, smiled as they walked up and stood in front of him.

The pastor perfectly performed the standard wedding vows. Gracie and Billy kissed, thanked him, and quickly walked out of the house and into the beautiful March afternoon. Rice began to pepper them as they ran to the waiting car with Just Married painted on the back window, and a noisy string of tin cans had been tied to the rear bumper. With Robert behind the steering wheel, they entered the backseat of the car. Billy rolled down the window and called out, "You are all invited to come by the apartment after dinner if you want."

A parade of cars sped down Main Street honking horns to let everyone know that a wedding had taken place. On the way back up Main Street, the parade passed a small yellow and white house. On the sidewalk in front of the house Allen Mitchell stood with a box of groceries in his arms ready for delivery to the elderly Mrs. Jenson. When he turned around to look at the parade, he thought he saw Gracie in the backseat of first car.

As the wedding car sped up the street, Gracie glanced out the window. Seeing Allen standing on the sidewalk, she cried out, "Oh geez, I forgot to break up with Allen!"

The young man that stood on the sidewalk stared in disbelief. The car that sped away from him had Just Married written in white paint across its trunk.

Gracie couldn't stop giggling as she ran up the stairs of the apartment. Billy yelled, "Wait for me!" while taking two stairs at a time behind her.

Reaching the front door, Gracie waited for Billy to catch up. "Are you going to carry me across the threshold?" she teased.

"Not this threshold," he answered. "When we have our own place in California I will."

"Okay, that's a deal," she answered.

Opening the front door, Gracie stopped abruptly. There on the sofa sat a smiling Edna and William. William rose from the sofa and walked over to his daughter. Uncharacteristically, he wrapped his strong arms around her and whispered apologizes for not making it to the wedding.

Edna spoke up. "We have an idea, and we wanted to share it with you. It's a wedding present. Come here and sit down so we can talk. Oh, and Miss Annie sent you a fried chicken dinner with her biscuits and gravy and Polk salad. Everything is in the kitchen."

William said, "Gracie, I know you have tickets to see Conway Twitty in St. Louis on April tenth, and we were thinking that you and Billy could stay here in the apartment until then. Edna will go with me back to Illinois. In two weeks we'll come back, take you to St. Louis, and you could go to the concert. We'll buy you tickets for the train from St. Louis to Redland so you can meet up with Nell and Larry. It would give you a little time to see MaMaw and PaPaw before you leave. It will be like a honeymoon in Garberville. Also, I want you to have this five hundred dollars to get you started. It'll provide you with the food you need now and help you get by until you find a job." He handed Billy a fat envelope.

Gracie rose from the chair and embraced her dad again. This gesture of love and concern coming from her daddy quickly healed years of anger stemming from what some people might have considered abuse. He was her daddy, and she wanted so much to forget and to forgive.

"Thank you, Daddy. I love you."

As Edna stood, Gracie let go of William and turned to her, gave her a hug, and whispered in her ear, "Thank you, Mom. I know this was your idea."

Turning to Billy, she asked, "What do you think, Billy?"

Billy shook his new father-in-law's hand. "Thank you, William. I think it's a very generous wedding present. I don't know what else to say except thank you, and yes, I will be careful with the money." Turning toward Gracie, he smiled. "We should go tell Mom and Larry. They think we're leaving with them tomorrow."

Edna walked over and placed her arm around William's waist. "Go on—we're going out to the farm and will leave you kids alone." We'll see you again in two weeks." Edna hugged Gracie and cried, "I'm going to miss you, my sweet girl."

When Billy told Larry and Nell about the plan to spend time in Garberville before going to California, they were happy. It would give them a chance to find a place and settle in before the young married couple arrived.

Gracie thanked Larry for all his efforts in making the quickie wedding happen. She could see the pride in his face when he said that his friend, the judge, was really the one to thank.

Billy didn't bother to ask his parents why they missed the wedding. When he mentioned it to Gracie later, he said that his mother didn't approve.

Gracie chattered continuously on the drive back to the apartment about the afternoon, the evening, and the surprise honeymoon. Billy drove quietly, already contemplating his plans for getting a job and a place of their own. The sense of his new responsibilities came to him quickly.

Later, coming cautiously out the bathroom in her pink nightgown, Gracie smiled at Billy lying across the bed looking handsome and happy. He motioned to her to come to the bed. In anticipation of what was coming, she took a deep breath and walked toward him.

Just as she reached the bed and took Billy's hand there was a knock on the front door. Still in his pajama bottoms, Billy jumped up and hurried to the living room. Gracie grabbed her robe and followed him. He opened the door. There on the landing were seven or eight of their best friends. Billy had invited them, and now they were here to celebrate and wish them well. The wedding night would have to wait, but that was okay.

Chapter 24

Monday, April 11, 1960
Southern Pacific Railway

The click-clack of the train and large roomy, comfortable seats lulled Gracie to sleep almost immediately after boarding.

A loud conversation between the two women in the seats across the aisle woke her up.

"I can't believe it. He's on this train. I went back there, and they told me to come on back after dinner. He may be talking to guests later. I'm going back there and plan to stay around until they let me in his private car."

Gracie leaned over to Billy and whispered, "Who are they talking about?"

"Elvis. He has a private car on the end of this train, and he's going all the way to California too."

"Can we go back and see him?" Gracie asked, trying to keep the excitement from her voice.

"I'll go back later and see what's going on. If it's okay, I'll come get you."

"Okay," Gracie said.

Gracie waited for Billy's return with excited anticipation. Finally, he came back to his seat, then plopped down next to Gracie saying, "No, you can't go back there. The only people around his car are several bodyguards and a couple of trampy women waiting around to see him."

"Oh, okay," Gracie said with clear disappointment in her voice.

"Are you hungry? We can go to the dining car and have some supper soon."

"Yes, I could eat. Can we afford it?"

Billy nodded. "I've made a budget and allowed for food on the train. I'll go to the restroom, and when I come back we'll go to the dining car."

As soon as Billy left the car, one of the women from across the aisle turned toward Gracie and asked, "Honey, I'm sorry for eavesdropping on your conversation, but why won't your brother let you go to Elvis's car? I'd tell him to mind his own business!"

Taken aback, Gracie jerked her head around facing a blond woman in an extremely short red paisley dress. Next to her, a younger woman dressed in a fashion strange to Gracie nodded in agreement. The young woman had flowers in her hair, many bracelets on her wrist, and colorful scarves hanging from her waist. Gracie found this attire strangely pleasing.

She scowled at the woman. "Billy is my husband, not my brother!"

"Oh, honey, that makes it even worse. Don't let him boss you around like that."

Gracie's body stiffened with resentment at the woman's reply. In a voice that was almost childlike, she announced, "He's my husband. I think he knows what's best for me."

"Oh, honey, you have a lot to learn," the young woman said sarcastically.

Sunday, May 22, 1960
Gracie's Grandmother Rudolph's House,
San Jose, California

As they sat in the backyard of the little white stucco house, in the shade of a plum tree, on the soft, cushiony dichondra grass lawn, Billy and Gracie talked about being in California, their new jobs, and their plans for the future.

Gracie's grandmother, a tiny elderly woman, opened the screen door and said, "Are you two hungry? I thought I would make a meat loaf for dinner."

"Grandma, we're going down to Ricardo's Pizza for dinner tonight. Billy has never had pizza."

"Alright," her grandmother said, then turned around and went back into the house, smiling.

"How do you know I'll like pizza?" Billy asked.

"Everyone likes pizza. You just wait—you'll love it. Besides, Rosie told me that the band that plays there is really good."

"A band?"

"Sure, many restaurants in San Jose have music every night. She told me about another place called The Basement. It's a coffeehouse with music and poetry. It's really in a basement of an old house. The two colored guys that sing there are supposed to be really good."

"Colored?"

"Yes, is that alright with you?"

"Yes, it's fine. I'm in California now. I like it that it's different here," he said.

Gracie smiled. "I'm glad you feel that way. I would like to go there sometime, but you don't drink coffee."

"I'm sure they have Coke too."

Suddenly Gracie whined, "Oh! I miss Missouri so much sometimes it makes me cry, but we can find all kinds of places to go and have fun so I won't miss the farm and our friends so much, right?"

"Right, but remember we have a budget. I've saved most of the money William gave us, so we should be able to get our own place in the next week or two."

Gracie looked up at him eagerly, "Oh, when can we start looking?"

"I thought we could look tomorrow. Your uncle John said he would drive us when we're ready."

Gracie leaned over and kissed Billy on the cheek. "I'm so excited. I can't wait. Let's go have some pizza and hear some music tonight and celebrate."

Chapter 25

Tuesday, June 21, 1960
San Carlos Street, San Jose

The transit bus pulled up to the curb. Billy put down his book, slowly walked to the bus, waited for the other passengers to enter, and then made his way in. Inside, he looked around and spotted a seat several rows back.

Before he arrived at the intended seat, though, a recognizable voice said, "Hey there, sit here with me."

Billy stopped and looked into the freckled face of the young man that had sat next to him on the bench at the bus stop.

For two weeks they never talked much, only exchanging a polite "hello" and "hi there."

Intimidated by the man's boldness, Billy started to move toward a seat at the back, but the man said again, "Here, this seat isn't taken."

"Thank you," Billy said as he sat down.

Billy was lonely. He was homesick. Homesick for Jerri, for his friends, the small-town atmosphere, and his freedom from worry. He didn't talk to Gracie about being homesick—she talked about it enough for both of them. Every day she mentioned that she wanted to go back to Garberville. When she told him she was pregnant, he sat her down and explained that the only way he could provide for a family was to stay in San Jose. She understood what he said, but she continued letting him know that she didn't like it. Billy kept quiet about his feelings and let her complain.

"I'm Ty," the young man offered.

"Billy," he said, pointing to his chest.

"You have an accent. Where are you from?" Ty asked.

"Missouri," Billy replied

"I have relatives in St. Louis."

"I'm from Garberville."

"I've never been to Missouri, but I hear it's very beautiful," Ty said

"Yes, it is nice," Billy said smiling at the thought Missouri.

"You don't talk much do you?" Ty said

"That's what they tell me," Billy said quietly.

"Welcome to California."

"Thank you. This is my stop."

"You're lucky you don't have to go far. Bye, Billy, see you at the bus stop tomorrow," Ty said smiling.

"Yes, well, uh, bye," Billy answered shyly.

Tuesday, June 21, 1960
Gracie and Billy's Apartment,
Richmond Street, San Jose

Rosie's red triumph sports car honked repeatedly as it came to a screeching stop in front of the dull-gray apartment building. Gracie hurried out of the building and immediately dropped her keys on the sidewalk. In her effort to pick them up, she dumped the contents of her purse onto the ground.

"Come on, girl—get your butt in this car before we're late for work," teased the little woman with the big voice.

"You just wait. I gotta pick this stuff up," Gracie yelled back.

"Girl, you haven't changed a bit. You're still as clumsy as ever."

"Well, maybe it's because I'm expecting."

"What!" Rosie screamed.

"Yes, I found out a few days ago." Opening the door to the Triumph, Gracie gave Rosie a quizzical look. "Now how am I supposed to get my long legs into this car, and can you please put the top up? I'm gonna mess up my hair."

"Stop complaining and just get in. You can comb your hair when we get to work. This car is the perfect size for me."

"Yeah, but you're tiny, and tiny I'm not."

"Hell, I'd rather be tall like you."

"Mutt and Jeff right? That's what everyone in school called us." They both laughed as the car engine roared and the tires squealed on takeoff.

"Rosie, did I thank you enough for getting me this job at Western Union?"

"Honey, you don't have to thank me. Isn't that what best friends are for?"

"Yes, but thank you anyway," Gracie said seriously.

"Hey, tell me about this expecting you just happened to mention," Rosie asked.

"I was using the rhythm method, but I guess it didn't work."

"Hell, Gracie, I could have told you that."

"Well, why didn't you?" Gracie said laughing.

Rosie turned her head and looked at Gracie, "I thought you would know about rubbers."

"We do, but Billy doesn't like them, and he doesn't like doing it much."

"Doing what?" Rosie asked obviously confused at what her friend was trying to say.

"You know!" Gracie said blushing.

Sex?"

"Yeah! But it's okay. I'm expecting now and I understand."

"What? Gracie, you're kidding right?" Rosie said loudly.

"No." Gracie answered obviously embarrassed.

Monday, June 27, 1960
San Carlos Street, San Jose

Standing, Billy tossed his cigarette into the gutter. "This bus has been late two days this week already."

"Yes, it gets tiresome, but at least it's given us a little more time to get acquainted," Ty said, smiling.

Billy ears began to warm as he recognized the flirtatious tone in Ty's voice. I like this man. He's funny, smart, and nice-looking, Billy thought. I do like seeing a friendly face at the bus stop every day.

"How did you get all the way from Garberville to San Jose?" Ty continued trying to make friendly conversation.

"Gracie and I took the train to Redlands, where my folks were staying," Billy said. "We didn't like it there. Gracie's uncle offered to let us stay with his family in San Jose until we got jobs. We took him up on the offer. We took the train again," Billy said.

"What are you doing at Sherman and Williams Paints? Ty asked.

The day after we arrived, we went to the employment office downtown. They said I scored high on a math test so Sherman and Williams gave me a job bookkeeping.

"Did your wife get a job?

"Gracie's friend from high school told her about an opening at Western Union, so we both have been working since our first week here. We moved into her grandmother's house for a few weeks because it was closer to our jobs. We rented our apartment two weeks ago. Everything has happened very fast. We have only been in California for a couple of months."   Darn, Billy thought, this man makes me nervous.

"Well, how about that. You can talk, can't you? How old are you, if I can ask a personal question like that?" Ty asked

Billy blushed more. "I'm nineteen."

"Nineteen? I'm twenty-nine and nowhere near ready to get married. You have a lot of responsibility."

"Maybe, but it's okay. I wanted to marry Gracie," Billy said, starting to feel a little more relaxed as he let this redheaded stranger know what his priorities were. "She wasn't expecting when we got married, but she is now. I found out a few days ago. I wish we would have waited, but it's too late now," Billy added just as the bus pulled up to the curb.

Billy entered the bus first. Standing behind him Ty thought, I want this handsome guy more than ever. I'll have to be very careful not to scare him. He's shy, but he likes me.

Chapter 26

Friday, July 15, 1960
Gracie and Billy's Apartment, San Jose

The only thing I have to drink is Coke," Billy said as he opened the front door of his apartment and the two men walked in.

Being aware for the first time how plain the apartment looked with its rented used furniture, the dingy green curtains, and no pictures on the walls, Billy said, "This apartment is only temporary—we plan on moving soon. I've almost enough saved for a better place."

Ty noticed Billy's embarrassment and said, "Hey, don't worry about it, everyone has to start somewhere." Quick to change the subject for Billy's sake, he asked, "Does Gracie like working the swing shift?"

"Not really, but it's only two to ten thirty, and she gets home at about eleven. Western Union sends her home in a taxi, and she has the morning to herself. It works out okay."

"I just happen to have some rum that I bought at lunchtime," Ty said as he pulled a small bottle from the inside pocket of his sport jacket. "I was going to take it home for a rum and Coke tonight. We could have this now."

"I have Coke in the fridge," Billy said as he walked into the tiny kitchen.

Two hours later, Billy swayed a little as he walked into the kitchen to pour another rum and Coke for Ty. "Whoa! I feel kinda wobbly. I better not have another," Billy said.

"Aw, come on—you only had two."

"Yeah, I know, but I've never had rum before. It's potent. I need to piss. I'll fix another when I get back."

Billy went into the bathroom and closed the door. When finished, he stepped in front of the sink and looked into the mirror, "Wow, I think I'm high," he said to his reflection.

When he heard the door open, his body became rigid. He didn't turn around. Ty walked up behind him, took him by the shoulders, and turned him around slowly.

As they came face-to-face Billy said, "No, Ty, don't, please don't."

Ty didn't want to hear this. He wanted to kiss Billy so badly he couldn't stop himself. He pulled Billy to him and kissed him.

The sensation from Ty's warm lips was so inviting that Billy gave in for a moment. Startled by this feeling of desire, Billy pushed him away and said again, "No, Ty. I said no."

6:30 pm
Friday July 15, 1960
Western Union Office

Gracie felt a shiver go down her back. She had an overwhelming feeling that something was terribly wrong. "What, is it? It's Billy," she realized. "Something's wrong with Billy. Gosh, I feel terrible. I think I'm going be sick," she said to herself, getting up from her chair. "Margaret, will you take over the switchboard? I'm going to the restroom. I feel bad."

"Go ahead, honey. What's wrong?" the blond coworker asked.

"I don't know—maybe I'm having morning sickness at night. I just feel weird."

Sitting on the toilet, Gracie's whole body begin to shake. "I wish we had a phone at the apartment so I could call. I need to go home! I can't stand this feeling, and it's getting worse."

Margaret called to Gracie from the bathroom door. "Honey, you okay in there?"

"No, I feel awful. I think I need to go home."

"Okay, dear. Your shift is almost over anyway. I'll call you a taxi."

As the taxi pulled into the apartment complex driveway, Gracie noticed a faint glimmer of light in the living room window.

Maybe I'm crazy, she thought. I'm sure Billy has already gone to bed and everything is fine.

Thanking the driver, she went to the front door. She heard the sound of voices inside her apartment, and stopped to listen, "Who is in there with Billy? The lights are low."

The taxi driver gave a friendly honk to Gracie as he backed out of the driveway. Startled Gracie jumped, grabbed the front door handle, opened it, and stepped in. Billy sat in the easy chair and the stranger sat on the sofa. Gracie noticed that they looked surprised and uneasy. Confused and feeling uncomfortable she stood statue-like in the open doorway. The sense of danger overwhelmed her. Feeling faint, she swayed and grabbed the doorframe. Billy rose from the chair and walked over to her, "What's wrong, are you alright?" he asked, taking her by the arm.

"I'm not feeling well. I needed to come home. I think I need to lie down."

The man on the sofa stood up. Billy noticed, "Gracie, this is Ty, he works near the paint shop. We met at the bus stop."

"Hello," said the short man with red hair.

"Hello," Gracie said. As she looked at this man, she realized right away that he was the source of her anxiety and fear. Feeling uncomfortable being in the same room with that person, she walked toward the bedroom door. "I need to lie down."

Gracie lay on her bed feeling helpless and confused. She could hear the two men talking but couldn't understand the conversation.

About an hour later, Billy opened the bedroom door and said, "I'm going to walk Ty to the bus stop. It's almost eleven thirty, and the last bus will be there soon."

"Okay."

Hours later, when Gracie heard the front door, open she glanced at the alarm clock on the dresser. "Oh my gosh, it's two a.m." Feeling grateful and relieved that Billy finally came home, Gracie started to cry.

Without turning on the light, Billy removed his clothing and crawled into bed. Reaching for Gracie, he moved closer and took her into his arms. Hearing her sniffles, he raised up on one elbow, "Gracie I'm so sorry. I didn't mean to worry you."

Overwhelmed with the feeling of fear and confusion again she started crying harder.

"Gracie, I'm sorry. I didn't mean to let this happen, but it was a good thing, honest. Look at me please."

Gracie turned over to face Billy. When she saw the sadness and sorrow in his eyes, she reached up and caressed his face. "What's wrong, Billy? What happened tonight?"

"I thought I might be a homosexual, but I proved tonight that I'm not. I'm not, Gracie, honest. I need to tell you something important." Not giving Gracie a chance to say anything more, Billy told her about his past. He told her about Bobby and the swimming secret at the river. He told her about how he had to threaten Bobby to get him to stay away. He confided in her about how hard it had been sometimes when he was lonely and feeling unloved not to let Bobby pull him back in. He told her that he was worried about being a homosexual because when all his friends were going steady, he never found a girl that he wanted.

At this point, he stopped talking, squeezed Gracie, and kissed the top of her head.

"Until you came to Garberville. I love you, Gracie. I found out tonight that I'm not homosexual. I want you, I want our baby, and I am so sorry I worried you tonight." Billy tightened his arms around her and softly began to cry, burying his face in her hair.

"Billy, it's okay, I love you. It's okay." Gracie said.

Several minutes later Gracie lifted herself up from the bed on one elbow and said, "Billy, I have a question. Can I ask you a question?"

Billy scooted his body back a little so he could look at her. "What's your question? I'll always be honest with you."

Gracie's young innocent face looked at him with a furrowed brow and said pleadingly, "What is a homosexual?"

Billy, with his face still wet with his tears, threw his head back and began to laugh. "Oh, my sweetheart, you are so naive."

Chapter 27

Friday, September 30, 1960
Gracie and Billy's Apartment
4th Street, San Jose, Ca

Lying in bed, Gracie placed her hands on her swollen stomach and thought, I'm so glad Billy found this apartment. It's so nice and in a much better neighborhood. I'm going to enjoy fixing up the baby's room. I can't believe we are so close to First Street and Dr. Stadler's office. I can walk to my appointments from here. Although there are no families in this complex the college guys across the way are friendly.

Billy, lying on his side with his back to Gracie, began breathing heavily. Obviously dreaming, he moaned, and then turned over vigorously, facing her.

Wanting to soothe him, Gracie reached over and softly rubbed his arm and back. Suddenly, with a jerk he moved toward her. Grabbing at her nightgown, he pushed it up around her breasts. Her lacy panties tore down the side during his efforts to pull them away. With a loud groan, he rolled over onto her and roughly entered her, yelling, "Bitch, bitch, bitch, I hate you." He quickly finished and turned back facing the wall. Without saying another word, his breathing became normal, and he was asleep again.

Gracie lay in bed dumfounded. Her mind went completely blank. She couldn't even think about what to do next. She lay there for hours just staring at the light and shadows on the bedroom walls.

A delicate movement in her belly, like the flutter of a butterfly's wings, startled Gracie from her stupor. The baby is moving! she thought. Still lying on the bed uncovered, with her nightgown crumpled under her breasts and her panties torn and wet at her side, she reached for a blanket to cover herself.

Suddenly, the realization of what happen came rushing back and she panicked. "The baby. Oh my gosh, the baby." She jumped up and rushed into the bathroom. Standing in front of the bathroom mirror, she looked for any bruises and felt around for sore spots. There were none. Calmly, she removed a clean nightgown from the bathroom drawer and put it on. She picked up a washcloth from the rack and wet it with hot water and applied soap. Very gently and with precision, she washed her face and body.

After tiptoeing into the bedroom, she crawled into the bed, turned her back toward Billy, and pulled the covers over her head. Exhausted, she immediately fell asleep.

The delicious smell of frying bacon and eggs filled the bedroom. Gracie sat up and looked around for Billy as she tried to clear her cloudy head.

Did I dream what happened? Oh my gosh, he hates me. What am I going to do? she thought as she got up, went out of the bedroom, and entered the kitchen.

Billy stood at the stove and turned when she came in. "I fixed eggs and bacon. Would you like some pancakes too?"

"No, eggs are enough," Gracie answered as she sat down at the table.

Billy set the eggs and bacon in front of her and stepped back. Looking down at her while she slowly began to eat, he thought, How can she sit there so calmly? Doesn't she want to discuss what happened? Is she afraid to know why it happened? Am I ready to confront her with the truth? I'm so sorry, I hope I didn't hurt her. It's not her fault. Damn, she should have some reaction and not sit there like nothing happened."

Gracie ate her breakfast in silence. Remembering how her daddy warned her not to cry or talk after he beat her, she thought it was best to be quiet and hope this would blow over. "Why did he make my breakfast? Maybe he's sorry. Maybe he doesn't know he did it," she thought.

Saturday, October 15, 1960
California Movie Theater,
San Jose

Walking out of the theater onto sidewalk, Gracie said wistfully, "I love Doris Day. Have you ever seen Calamity Jane?"

"No, I can't say that I have," Rosie answered. "I don't usually see romantic comedies."

"Oh, I do. I love them. I like happy stuff," Gracie said, buttoning her coat, and then wrapping her arms around her swollen belly.

"I know, I know, you're Miss Cheerful," Rosie said, smiling at her friend. "Hey, since we're on First Street, let's go to the Karmel Korn shop. It's just down the block, and my friend Jim works there," she suggested.

Gracie stopped smiling abruptly. "Well, I should be going home. Billy may be home by now, and I forgot to leave a note. He won't know where I am."

Rosie frowned and turned to Gracie. "Who cares? He hasn't been home on time for days, and you don't know where he's been. You told me he doesn't come home until midnight sometimes."

Gracie looked down and turned her face away in an effort to hide the pain she felt from Rosie's harsh but truthful words. "He's working overtime doing inventory," Gracie answered in Billy's defense.

Rosie, seeing that she had upset her friend, didn't say anything more. Taking Gracie's arm, Rosie pulled her in the direction of the Karmel Korn shop. "Come on, girl—no frowns tonight. You'll like Jim. He's a great guy."

"Yummm, it smells wonderful in here," Gracie said upon entering the Karmel Korn shop.

"Not if you work here and smell it for hours every day," the very tall, lanky young man said with a smile.

"Gracie, this is Jim Smith; Jim, this is my friend Gracie."

"Hi there."

"Hi."

"We just came from the movies, and I thought we could use a snack. Gracie lives down on Fourth Street now. She walks to the coffee shop on the corner at San Carlos almost every night. In her condition, I thought she should know someone that works around here," Rosie explained.

"Welcome. Here, Gracie, you look like you need to sit." He dragged a stool from the corner of the small room.

"Oh yeah, pay attention to the cute pregnant woman and ignore the friend," Rosie said, laughing.

With the uneasy feeling that she needed to go home, but reluctant to say anything, Gracie sat on the stool listening to the small talk between the two friends. After twenty minutes or more, she felt she couldn't wait any longer and told Rosie she needed to leave.

"Okay, let's get you home before you turn into a pumpkin. Oh, wait a minute—you already have," Rosie teased.

Jim laughed and then apologized. "I'm sorry to laugh Gracie, but Rosie is funny."

Still chuckling, he handed Gracie a small bag of Karmel Korn, saying, "Anytime you're downtown, come on by. I enjoy the company. The owner says we must stay open until eleven even though we don't have many customers that late."

Wednesday, October 19, 1960
First Street Coffee Shop, San Jose, CA

The waitress asked, "Do you want me to heat up that coffee again?"

"Yes, please," Gracie answered, just as the bus pulled up to the stop across the street from the twenty-four-hour coffee shop. Gracie's heart raced as she watched out the window at each person descending the bus. When the doors to the bus closed and no Billy in sight, hot tears filled her eyes and she began to cry softly. In an effort to stop crying she swallowed hard several times, grabbed her jacket, wiggled out of the booth, and said a little too loudly, "Why am I doing this again? This is stupid. He's not coming home. I've got to get out of here."

Seeing her stumble a little on the way to the door, the waitress asked Gracie, "Honey, are you okay?"

"Yes, yes," was all she managed to say.

Standing outside the restaurant, not knowing what to do now, and not wanting to go home to an empty apartment, she walked down First Street toward the Karmel Korn shop.

Jim smiled when he saw Gracie through the glass door. He said, "Hi there, pretty lady."

"Hi, hope I'm not bothering you," she answered.

"No, never. It's closing time, and I have to clean these machine before I go home. Make yourself comfortable."

With that, Gracie sat on the stool and started to relax while watching him work. The conversation started out with Jim asking her bluntly, "Why are you out at night by yourself?"

His bluntness surprised her. She answered him with, "I'm uncomfortable and can't sleep, so I walk at night until I get sleepy." Trying to change the subject, she asked, "Rosie told me you were going to San Jose State and you're dating Maureen Parks—is that true?"

"No, we broke up a couple of weeks ago."

"Oh, I'm sorry. I only asked because I went to grammar school with Maureen and we were friends. Kind of. We talked to each other at school."

"Really? Well, that's okay. We were together for two years. Now I'm busy trying to finish my education and trying not to think about it," Jim said, obviously not thrilled about the breakup. "Gracie, I'm not buying that you are just out walking around," he said, changing the subject.

At first, she started to make another excuse, but she was still feeling so distraught that she decided to tell him the truth.

"We moved downtown few weeks ago and Billy started to stay away a lot at night. He gets mad at me when I asked him why he comes home so late. His explanation is that he was doing inventory and getting paid overtime," she explained.

"Really?" Jim asked.

"When I asked him to call me if he is going to be late he told me that there is some kind of short in the electrical system and when the heater comes on at night it interferes with the phone," Gracie said with her head down, knowing full well that this sounded untrue.

Realizing that the husband of this sweet girl was lying to her Jim felt his face get hot, Damn, he thought, is she so naive that she doesn't know or simply did doesn't want to believe that her husband is being deceitful. It doesn't feel right sending her away when she feels so obviously unhappy.

I can walk you home as soon as I finished cleaning the equipment and close the shop. I live on 6th street," Jim said,

Twisting the gold band on her finger, Gracie said, "I don't think so. It might upset Billy,"

"Oh, come on. We're both going in the same direction."

"Okay," Gracie answered, feeling relieved that Jim didn't seem annoyed at her for dumping her unhappiness on him.

Chapter 28

Thursday, December 29, 1960
Gracie and Billy's Apartment

Wobbling into the room heavily pregnant, Gracie found Billy staring at their wedding picture. "What are you doing?" she asked.

Not looking at her, he said, "I need to talk to you."

"What?" she asked.

Billy turned and motioned for her to sit down. He took her hand and helped her into the chair. He pulled a kitchen chair into the living room and placed it so that he faced Gracie.

"I know I haven't been fair leaving you alone and not telling you the truth about where I've been. I know you've been unhappy, and I'm sorry. It's killing me, but now I must be honest because I can't go on like this for another minute."

Gracie stared at Billy with a look of fear and confusion. She sensed what he was about to say, and she didn't want to hear it.

"Remember when I told you that I thought I was homosexual, but when Ty made a pass at me I turned him down?"

Gracie said, "Yes."

"Well, there is a nickname for homosexuals, it's called being Gay. I can't keep it from you any longer, I am Gay. I didn't know it then, but I know it now. I've been lying to you, and I can't do it anymore. I want to move out. I'll still take care of you and anything you need, but I just can't live here. I'm in love with Ty, and I want to live with him. If I don't live with him, he says he'll leave me."

Gracie's mind suddenly became dark. She could hear what he was saying, but she had a hard time processing it. The words "I'm in love with someone" rang in her ears. She tried to listen very carefully as he explained that he fell in love with Ty soon after the night she came home early and found him in their apartment.

Seeing the confusion in her eyes, Billy asked, "Are you listening?" When she didn't answer, he waited a few moments and then went on with his explanation. He told her the apartment they were living in now had once belonged to Ty and that he lived only two blocks away on 5th Street. He explained that all the times he told her that he needed to go for a walk to clear his head, he went to Ty's apartment and had sex. He talked about how he felt that his relationship with Bobby had brought out his homosexual tendencies. He made it clear that Ty was the first man he had felt close to since Bobby.

Gracie just sat there listening, not saying anything. When Billy stopped talking, he asked, "Do you understand?"

"Not all of it. I want to call my parents and tell them we're splitting up."

"You can't tell them I'm homosexual," Billy said with fear in his voice.

"I know, I won't tell them. I'll just say we can't get along and that I want to leave. I'll tell them I'm unhappy."

"Gracie, I'm sorry. We're so young, and we know so little about sex. I didn't know I was Gay when we got married. All I knew was that I loved you, and honestly, I still do. I don't want to lie anymore. It's killing me. It's really killing me. Talk to me, help me, help you."

Gracie, realizing what this confession meant to her future, began to cry.

Sobbing, she said, "I've been miserable too. Especially after . . . you know what. I thought there should be more affection, but I didn't know for sure. I thought something was wrong with me for wanting more, and I didn't know how to ask you. I guess I should have read some books or something. I don't want to talk anymore. I want to call my parents and ask them to come to California."

Billy stood, went to the table, picked up the phone, and handed it to Gracie.

Chapter 29

Sunday, January 15, 1961
El Rancho Drive-In Theater, San Jose

The movie was over. Jim rolled down the window, put the speaker back on its rack outside, and rolled the window up again. "We should wait until some of the cars leave—it will be easier."

"Okay. That was a fun movie. Thank you for bringing me," Gracie replied, turning toward Jim and giving him a huge smile.

"I like going to the drive-in, but I don't like going by myself, and besides—you're good company. Would you like to go to dinner on Friday?" he asked.

"I'd like that, but are you sure you want to be seen with a big-bellied pregnant woman?"

"A sweet, pretty pregnant woman," Jim answered.

Looking at Jim, Gracie asked, "Seriously, is it like a date?"

"Let's just say for now that we are two friends taking care of each other," Jim said.

"That sounds right," Gracie said, relieved that it wasn't becoming complicated.

Jim started the car and pulled away from the space. "I'm sorry for what happened between you and Billy. It's great that your mom and dad decided to get an apartment in San Jose to help you out. I would have worried if you had tried to do this by yourself."

"My mom and dad want me to go back to Missouri with them, but the doctor said I couldn't travel. Besides, I wouldn't be alone. Rosie and her mom would have helped me out," Gracie said.

"It's good to have friends like that around," Jim said.

"Rosie is the best," Gracie said with a smile.

Tuesday, February 14, 1961
Edna and William's Apartment
Moorpark Avenue, San Jose

Gracie roamed around the little apartment wishing her parents would get home from work soon. She had strange sharp pains in her stomach and felt anxious about being alone.

Going to the bedroom window, she looked out at the rows and rows of apartment buildings along the street. They were all the same two-story plain brown or gray, and with no real landscape, and nobody on the sidewalks. Looking down the street, she didn't see anyone walking around the neighborhood. She felt a little panic as the pain in her stomach became sharper. From her vantage point, she couldn't see the bus stop, but if she bent her head far to the left, she could see part of the sidewalk that led to her apartment building. Finally, she saw her mother walking toward their apartment from the bus stop. Hurrying, she went into the living room, opened the front door, and waited for Edna to come around the corner.

"What's wrong?" Edna said, seeing the look on Gracie's face.

"I'm having funny pains and today is my due date," Gracie said excitedly.

"Have you timed your pains?"

"No, I wanted to wait until you came home."

"Well, get the stopwatch in the drawer and start timing."

An hour or so later William came in the front door. Finding Gracie sitting on the sofa with his stopwatch, he asked, "What's going on? Is it time?"

"No, not yet" Edna said. "Gracie thought she was having some pains, but nothing has happened for an hour. I think she's excited about it being her due date. Besides, she said all she ate today were four honey-and-butter sandwiches. I think enough to make anyone have stomach pains," Edna said as she gave William a look and a smile—the kind of smile that a mother has when her child does something cute and endearing.

February 17, 1961
San Jose Hospital, San Jose

Gracie held the soft bundle in her arms. She looked lovingly at the small miracle with a dark face, slanted brown eyes, and black hair, and said, "Her hair is so black."

Billy laughed and said, "William asked me if I thought you'd been fooling around with a Japanese person."

"He said that?"

"Yes, but you know him—he was just kidding. You still want to name her Mary Lynne?"

"Yes, isn't that what we agreed? They're going to put a cast on her foot tomorrow," Gracie said, pulling the blanket away and looking at the tiny foot pressed tight against the baby's leg. "The doctor said we're lucky that it wasn't more of a clubfoot. Sometimes the foot is more deformed, but hers is almost normal. Dr. Sattler said it happened because I don't have much room to carry a baby. She kicked me constantly with that foot. I think it was hung up under my ribs for a long time."

Billy got up from the chair and walked over to Gracie. "I have to go. I'll be back tomorrow." He leaned down and kissed her on the cheek. "You did a good job."

At that moment, the door to Gracie's room opened, and Jim walked in holding a very large teddy bear and bouquet of red roses. He stopped abruptly when he saw Billy. "Am I intruding?" Jim asked, glancing at Billy.

Gracie gave him a big smile. Excited to see him, she answered, "No, not at all. Come see my baby."

Turning toward Billy, Jim said, "Hi."

"Hi Jim," Billy said without smiling.

He set the flowers and bear on the table near the bed, walked over, and looked down at the sleeping infant. Billy sat down again.

"How are you?" Jim asked.

"I'm okay, but still tired."

"Did you have a hard time?"

"Yes, it took thirty-six hours. Thank you for the bear and flowers."

"You're very welcome, but I can't stay. I have a class in a few minutes, but I wanted to see how you were feeling."

"I'm fine."

"Okay, I'll talk to you later."

"I'll be here four more days. Will you come by again?" Gracie asked.

Jim looked at Billy and said, "I'll call and see when it's a good time."

Seeing the sadness on Jim's face Gracie said, "Okay, please do."

Chapter 30

Thursday, March 30, 1960
Billy and Ty's Apartment
5th Street, San Jose

Billy was sitting on the sofa with his eyes closed listening to Johnny Mathis singing "Maria," when Ty walked into the living room and asked, "Why are you so quiet today?"

"I didn't realize I was being quiet. I'm just listening to the music."

"Believe me, you haven't said two words to me all day," Ty responded.

"The truth is I've been thinking about the baby," Billy said, sounding a little irritated.

"Oh, is something wrong with her?"

"Not that I know of, but I haven't had a chance to see her for two weeks, so I went by Gracie's apartment today. She wasn't home. She took the baby and went somewhere with Rosie. I couldn't see her yesterday because Gracie and Rosie went to Santa Cruz with some friends. There were men in the car."

"How do you know there were men?" Ty asked.

"I drove to the apartment and saw them going around the corner in a blue car. There was a man driving. I called Edna and asked to speak to Gracie, and she told me she had gone to Santa Cruz."

"Are you upset about not seeing the baby, or are you upset about Gracie going to Santa Cruz with men?"

Billy sat in silence for a long while. "I would like to see my baby."

"I'm not sure I believe you," Ty said loudly as he left the living room and went into the kitchen.

Saturday, June 18, 1961
Western Union Office

"Where do you want to go for lunch today?" Gracie asked as she walked out of the Western Union office. "I only have an hour. I was a little late last time you took me to lunch."

"Let's go to the coffee shop on the corner at First and San Carlos. Do you know the one I mean?" Billy asked, taking her hand to help her cross the street.

"Yes, I'm very familiar with that coffee shop," Gracie said a little bitterly.

"Oh yes. I'm sorry," Billy said in a low voice.

Gracie walked up to a booth and slid across the well-worn seat, settling close to the window. A shiver went up her spine as she looked out at the familiar bus stop. How many times did I sit in this exact same spot waiting for Billy to come home? she thought.

Billy slid in on the other side. The waitress with the bright-red hair came sauntering over to take their order.

"I would like a BLT and a Coke," Gracie said.

"I'd like the same thing and a ashtray please," Billy said.

"Why did you want to have lunch today?" Gracie asked.

"You get right down to it, don't you?" Billy took her hand, smiling. "I wanted to ask you if it would be possible for me to bring Edna to my house for a weekend. I never get to spend enough time with her."

"No! Never," Gracie said. Her response was so loud, all the people in the café turned to see who said it.

"Why not? I can take care of her as good as anyone can," Billy pleaded.

"You are not taking her to that place where Ty lives," Gracie said. Her anger was obvious by the shrillness in her voice.

"Please don't be upset. I am just trying to find a way to spend time with her, nothing more."

"You can come to our apartment," Gracie offered.

"It's always hard to spend time with Mary when William and Edna are there. They don't like me," Billy said.

"Don't be silly—they care about you," Gracie said.

"It doesn't feel that way. I think your dad knows what's going on." Billy's cheeks turned pink as he took the cigarette pack from his shirt pocket, removed one, and tapped the end on his wrist. He turned and looked around for an ashtray. He lit the cigarette and took a long, deep drag of the smoke.

The waitress came to the table with their lunch, set it down, and started to walk away. "Do you have an ashtray?" Billy asked again.

"Oh, yes." She reached into her apron pocket and set the large ashtray on the table between them.

"Thank you," Billy said, flicking the ash into the ashtray.

"Why don't you come over to our apartment and stay this weekend. I don't have to work, and my mom and dad are going to be away. You can take care of the baby, and I will finally get some sleep."

"I can do that. I can take care of her," Billy said excitedly.

"Well, I have one more request."

"What is it?"

"You must cook chicken and dumplings for dinner Saturday night." Gracie smiled teasingly.

"Oh, now that sounds like blackmail." Billy smiled back.

"Call it what you want, I'm sooooo hungry for your chicken and dumplings."

Later that night, Billy told Ty his plans.

Ty yelled, "What do you mean you're staying in Gracie's apartment and taking care of the baby this weekend?"

"Just what I said. I can't bring Mary here so I'm going there. I'm going over Friday night and staying all weekend so I can get to know my baby. It's the only way it will work."

"Will Gracie be there?" Ty asked.

"Of course, but you know it will be okay. It's better for the baby if we learn to be friends."

"I don't like it, and you can just forget about it. You are not going to do it, and that's that!" Ty said, spitting the words out.

"What? Are you really telling me I can't go?" Billy asked.

"Yes, that's what I'm telling you," Ty said flatly.

"If you think you're going to keep me from my child, you're crazy. I've let you tell me what to do and what not to do long enough. You try to stop me, and I will leave for good," Billy yelled as he exited the room.

Saturday, June 24, 1961

"You can sleep in my room with Mary and I'll sleep in Mom and Dad's room. The diapers and stuff are all on that changing table," Gracie said as Billy followed her into the bedroom. "She's sleeping now, but it won't be long until she wakes up. Let's go into the kitchen and have a Coke."

"I brought some groceries," Billy said.

"You did?" Gracie said, surprised.

"Yes, I got orders from someone to make chicken and dumplings tomorrow night." Billy looked at her seriously.

"I was just teasing," Gracie said.

"I know, I know, but I wanted to," Billy said.

Billy watched Gracie as she sat on the sofa looking through a magazine and sipping a Coke through a straw. He marveled at her ability to forgive him and allow him to be here with their baby. As he looked at her, he thought of how much he loved her and wondered if he had made the right choice in leaving his family.

She looked up and smiled. "What are you thinking?" she asked.

"I'm grateful that you asked me to come over this weekend," he said.

"Well, I want us to be friends. It's best for Mary. Besides, Mom's gone, and you cook better than I do," she teased.

Chapter 31

Sunday Afternoon, August 6, 1961

"I've enjoyed these weekends with you and Mary," Billy said on his way out the door of Gracie's apartment.

"Me too. I like getting some sleep when you take over," Gracie said, grinning.

"I want us to be together all the time. I want my family together," Billy said wishfully.

Stunned, Gracie only managed to reply, "What?"

"Do you understand? I want you, me, and Mary to have our own place and be a family."

Gracie stammered, "I can't talk right now. Call me later and we'll talk about it, but I don't think so."

With that, Gracie closed the door, leaving Billy on the step outside. The baby whimpered in the bedroom. Gracie rushed into the room and picked her up. Holding the wiggling child close, she whispered in her ear, "Oh goodness, baby, your daddy wants to live with us."

Gracie fed Mary and soon after the baby went to sleep in her arms. She gently put Mary in her bassinette and covered her with a soft blanket. Crawling on her bed, she curled up into the fetal position and went to sleep.

Gracie awoke to the sound of sizzling chicken fried steak as Edna cooked dinner in the kitchen. It smells real good, I'm glad they are home, she thought.

From where she was sitting on the edge of her bed she could see William relaxing in the easy chair reading the evening paper and commenting occasionally on an issue he wanted to share with anyone in earshot. She reached into the crib next to her bed and stroked the sleeping baby's soft brown hair as she thought about what to do.

Mom and Dad want me to go back to Missouri and live on the farm with MaMaw and PaPaw. I know it's the sensible thing to do, but even though I miss them terribly, it just doesn't feel right. My salary at Western Union will barely pay for an apartment in San Jose, and Billy can only afford to help me pay for some of the things the baby needs. It would be better if Billy and I could work it out. It would be better for the baby. Does he really want to get back together? Does he want to be husband and wife, or does he just want to live as friends? What does he want to do?

The phone rang in the living room. Gracie's heart started beating fast. "That's your daddy," she said to the sleeping infant. She could hear Edna answering, "Hello? Yes, she's here."

Putting the phone down, Edna called, "Gracie, it's Billy."

Thursday, August 31, 1961
Western Union

Gracie walked out of Western Union office, looked up, and marveled at beauty of the magnolia tree just across the street. It was a beautiful day, and Gracie felt light and happy. She couldn't wait to get back to their new apartment and start dinner for Billy. Everything had fallen into place. Her mom and dad were going back to Missouri, leaving Gracie and Billy alone to start a new life together. Anyone that took the time to watch her walk down the street would know that this young woman was very happy.

"Hi, Gracie," came a voice from the shadows of the doorway next door to Western Union.

"Oh, Ty! You startled me."

"Sorry, I waited here out of the sun for your shift to end so I could talk to you again."

"I told you I don't think our little talks, and keeping it from Billy, is a good idea," Gracie said as she walked on, picking up a little speed.

Ty caught up to her and took her arm. "Gracie, you have to understand that we both love him and he loves us both. We can work out something that will make him happy. I know we can."

Gracie not so gently removed his hand from her arm and said, "I don't want us all to live together and that is that, Ty. Just go away and leave us alone."

He stepped in front of her and grabbed both arms this time. "I understand why Billy finds it hard to leave you. I think I've fallen in love with you too. I know we could be a happy family. I just know it. If you would just give it a chance. We all could be happy. Gracie, I love you too."

Gracie pulled away from his grasp. "What? You're crazy—leave me alone." Quickly she turned and hurried to the bus stop.

Luckily, the bus pulled up to the stop just as she got there. Gracie quickly entered.

Just before she was all the way in the bus, Ty yelled, "Billy is a gay. He will always be a homosexual. You are going to be sorry—just wait and see!"

Chapter 32

Saturday, October 14, 1961
Lake Tahoe, CA

"Sure is beautiful here," Billy said, pulling Gracie to his side. They stood alongside the road at the scenic overlook for a few minutes, soaking up the beauty of the valley below.

"I'm so happy Mom and Dad suggested we go to Tahoe before they leave for Missouri," Gracie said, tucking her body tightly under Billy's arm.

"They wanted an excuse to have Mary for a while before they leave," Billy said, smiling.

"I think you're right. Mom sure likes babysitting Mary. I'm sure she would keep her day and night if I let her."

Abruptly Billy turned Gracie around to face him. "I know I haven't been a good husband, and you've waited for me to be ready so patiently. I appreciate that. I love you, and I'm ready to be with you. I want to have another baby."

Shocked at Billy's bluntness, Gracie said, "Really? So soon?"

Yes, I would like one more child to complete our family," he said sincerely.

Surprised and having some doubt, Gracie looked up and searched his face. Seeing only love, hope, and sincerity—all the things she wanted from her husband—she took his hand and said shyly, "Let's go back to our cabin and talk it over."

"Wait—one more thing. I bought you a little present. Every time you doubt me I want you to play it," Billy said as he pulled the small disc from his jacket pocket. When she read the label, "Daddy's Home," Gracie threw her arms Billy's waist, laid her head on his chest, and mumbled, "Thank you, but for a while I may have to play it every day to believe it."

Sunday, November 5, 1961
Hillsdale Avenue, San Jose

Arm in arm they walked out the front door of the pretty yellow ranch-style house. Edna said, "I think this will work. The arrangement of the bedrooms will provide privacy for us. Gracie and Billy can have the two bedrooms at the end by the kitchen, and we can take the master bedroom."

"Yes, it'll be fine," William said.

Edna stopped, looked up at William, and said, "I really think we're making the right decision. I can't leave Gracie pregnant, not knowing for sure that Billy won't leave her again."

"I know. I'm worried too. I'm glad you made the suggestion. Everything will work out all right. I have plenty of work here. Track homes are going up like crazy, and with Billy's new job at Castle and Cook, he can afford to pay half the rent," he assured her.

"Thank you for understanding. They're still so young and need our help," she said as she wrapped both arms tightly around his waist.

He kissed Edna on top of her head. "I'm going back to work. You can go back to the apartment and tell the kids we found a place to live. I'll be home for dinner."

Thursday, June 21, 1962

Edna pulled two suitcases from under the bed and placed them on top. Opening the middle drawer of the dresser, she frantically pulled out panties, slips, and underwear. After tossing them haphazardly into the smaller of the two suitcases, Edna opened the bottom drawer, removed all of William's underwear, and flung them into the case saying, "You fool."

Gracie stood in the doorway. "Mom, what's going on? What are you doing?"

"Your damn father is at it again. He's been sleeping with Bob's wife, Sue. Bob has a gun and he's looking for William. He swears he's going to shoot him. What decent man sleeps with his best friend's wife?"

"Where's Daddy, is he alright?"

"He's hiding out somewhere. I'm supposed to meet him at the Catholic Church parking lot on Willow Street. Your uncle Jim will pick up the car and bring it back to you. We're going to Missouri in the truck." Edna opened the closet door, grabbed an armful of clothing, stuffed it all into the large suitcase, and slapped it shut. "We'll call when we're settled, and you can send us the rest of this stuff."

"Where will you go? Are you going with Daddy?" Gracie asked.

"I don't know. I really don't know," Edna replied, "We can't go to the farm—Bob will find us there."

Gracie rubbed her swollen pregnant belly, "Mom, you won't be here when the baby is born!"

From her crib, Mary started screaming,"Ganny, Ganny."

"I'm sorry. I'm sorry, but I have to go. Bob will shoot him. I'm sure of it," Edna said as she pulled the suitcases off the bed and walked toward the door.

Gracie moved out of the way and let her pass. When she heard the front door slam, she rushed into her daughter's room. Lifting Mary from the crib, Gracie held the toddler tight against her body, "Shhh, it's alright, baby. It's alright," she said, burying her face in her baby's soft brown curls.

Mary's tiny arms reached out toward the front door. "Ganny, Ganny!" she cried.

Chapter 33

Sunday, June 24, 1962, 8:30 p.m.
O'Connor Hospital, San Jose

Leaning over to give Gracie a kiss good-bye, Billy said, "My mom and Larry are supposed to arrive in a couple of days, and I need to buy some groceries before they get to the house. I'm going to leave now and pick you up in the morning."

"Are they all coming?" Gracie asked.

"Yes. Remember—we talked about this. Larry got laid off a couple of days ago, but he's already lined up a job in San Jose. They'll stay with us until they find a place to live," Billy answered.

"Please stay with me. I want you to be here when I have the baby!" Gracie exclaimed.

"The doctor said it's not time yet. It's false labor, but he won't release you until tomorrow morning," Billy soothingly whispered as he pushed Gracie's bangs away from her eyes. "We'll just have to wait a little longer for our baby to be born."

"Oh yeah! Maybe you can wait a while longer, but I'm tired of being a moose!" she whined. "I'm having this baby tonight. You can count on it!"

Billy sighed. "I'm going home now. I'll be here at nine thirty in the morning. The nurse said they would release you at ten. On our way home we can pick up Mary at Aunt Flo's house."

Billy went to the door. and turned around. Ignoring Gracie's pouting lips, he blew her a kiss.

Monday, June 25, 1962, 3:00 a.m.

The harsh ringing woke Billy from a deep sleep. As he reached for the phone on the bedside table, a framed photo fell onto the carpet. He ignored the photo and said, "Hello?"

"May I speak to Billy Baxter?"

"Yes, I'm Billy."

"I'm Nurse Laura at the San Jose Hospital. Your wife is in labor. She hasn't gone into the delivery room yet, but it won't be long."

"Okay, okay, thank you, I'll be right there." As Billy hung up the phone, he looked down and noticed the upside–down frame on the carpet by the bed. He picked it up, stared for a moment at the smiling girl in the photograph, and said, "Gracie, Gracie! You are always full of surprises."

Monday, June 25, 1962 1:30 p.m.

Billy walked into his house and went directly to the refrigerator, opened it, and said as he scanned the inside, "Damn, I forgot to get eggs. I'll have to go back to the store." He grabbed a Coke and set it on the counter, reached into his shirt pocket, took out a package of cigarettes, removed one, lit it, and took a deep draw. He let the smoke out slowly. From the counter he picked up a folded piece of paper with the phone number of the motel where Edna and William were staying. He turned toward the wall phone and sighed. Damn William! Edna should be here, he thought. He picked up the phone and began to dial.

"Hello, Jacksonport Motel," said a husky voice.

"I'd like to talk to Edna Meriwether. She's in room 6—it's an emergency," Billy said.

"Who's calling?" the voice asked.

"Her son-in-law," Billy replied.

"Okay, just a minute, I'll go get her."

Billy opened the Coke and began to take a drink, when a frantic voice said, "Hello, Billy—what's wrong? Is Gracie all right?"

"Yes, she's fine. She had a baby girl last night," he answered.

"It's too soon! Is the baby all right?" Edna asked.

"Yes, the baby is three weeks early. She's very tiny—five pounds, one ounce—but the nurse said she's otherwise perfect. She has strawberry-blond hair and big eyes that seem to cover her whole face. Her little legs are the same size as my thumbs. We're going to name her Krystal Lyn. The nurse let me hold her, and she made a little smile. But the nurse said it was just a gas bubble," Billy said, talking excitedly.

"Thank goodness! I would love to see her. How's Mary? I miss her so much," Edna said.

"She's fine. She is staying with Aunt Flo until Gracie comes home. She misses you too. She asks about you all the time," Billy said.

He could hear the sniffling on the other end of the line. "Everything will be okay Edna. I'll call you in a couple of days and let you know how they're doing," Billy said.

"Damn William! I should be there," Edna said, the anger and pain oozing through the phone.

"Edna, I'm very tired. I've gotta go and get some rest."

"You go ahead, Billy, but call me again soon. You know me—I'll worry until I talk to Gracie," Edna said.

"I promise. I'll have her call you as soon as she's able," he reassured her.

Billy laid the phone in the cradle and started to walk away, when it rang loudly.

"Hello," he answered. "Damn, I'll leave right away," he said.

San Jose Hospital, San Jose

Billy reached the hospital in record time, parked the car, and rushed into the hospital. Once he reached the maternity unit, he stopped and took a deep breath before going to the nurse's station. He saw a smile and look of recognition on the attending nurse's face as he walked toward her. "Mr. Baxter, your wife is out of surgery already and in Room 204."

"Is my wife all right?" Billy asked.

"Doctor Cunningham is in the room with her right now. You should ask him."

Billy hurried down the hall to Room 204 and entered.

Dr. Cunningham turned and faced him, "Hello there. Your wife gave us quite a scare, but everything is fine now. Gracie had a hematoma about the size of a small orange under the stitches. We removed it, and now she's as good as new."

"What's a hematoma?" Billy asked.

"It's a blood clot," the doctor said."The nurse wouldn't believe me when I told her I couldn't move because it hurt too much. I was lucky that Dr. Cunningham came in just as the nurse was yelling at me for being a sissy," Gracie said angrily.

"Yes, it was unfortunate that the nurse chose those words for someone in pain. I have taken care of the situation, and Gracie has a new nurse," Dr. Cunningham replied.

Billy walk to Gracie's bedside and took her hand. "I'm sorry I didn't stay and keep you company. I was so tired, and I have to work tomorrow," Billy said.

"It's alright. You didn't know, and besides, you look awful. Have you had any sleep?" Gracie asked.

"I slept for a couple of hours before they called me at three a.m., but nothing since."

"Billy, your hands are shaking. Please go home and sleep. I'll be in good hands with the doctor. Honest," Gracie pleaded.

"Okay. Mom and Larry won't be here for a couple of days after all, so it will be a good time for me to sleep. It's okay to call me if anything else happens," Billy said, taking a deep breath.

"She'll be fine; don't worry, I'll call you," the doctor assured Billy.

Chapter 34

Friday, December 22, 1963
Gracie and Billy's Duplex,
Whitehall Ave., San Jose

"We did it! That's the last load. I'm so tired. We have no kids tonight, so let's get hamburgers for dinner," Gracie said, plopping down hard on the sofa.

"We still have to put everything away," Billy said, looking at the many boxes scattered around the room.

"I know. If we get the beds made up, I can empty the boxes gradually."

"The girls come home in the morning. You won't be able to get much done, so I'm going to take off work tomorrow. It should take me only one day to have it organized," Billy said.

"Billy, I love our little duplex. I'm very excited about living so near to Bascom Avenue. Everything is so familiar. It's right in the middle of where I lived when I was in high school," Gracie said.

"There are a lot of couples our age that live on this street of duplexes. We should be able to meet some people our age," Billy said.

"I hope so, but you know me, I'm shy when it comes to meeting people," Gracie said.

"It's a nice neighborhood, don't you think?" Billy said.

Gracie stood, walked over to Billy, sat in his lap, and said, "Yes, it really is. I'm happy that you found this nice place and now we will be living alone again. I hope we can stay here for a long time."

Placing his arms around her, Billy laid his head on her shoulder, "I know it was hectic having our new baby and living with my family, but I think everyone handled it well. Now we have our own place and no more living with family, yours or mine, right?"

"Right," Gracie said.

Friday, May 10, 1963

The blond baby girl giggled when Gracie picked her up from the crib.

"Oh, your diaper is soaked and your clothes are wet."

She turned, grabbed a little blanket, a clean diaper, and t-shirt from the end of the bed, and walked into the living room with the wiggling baby. She spread the blanket on the sofa, laid the baby on the blanket, and proceeded to take off the wet clothes. The baby, started to cry.

"Shhhhh, Mary is still sleeping….shhhhh. Peek-a-boo, peek-a-boo," Gracie played with Kris, hoping to distract her from crying. She responded with a giggle. Gracie picked up a rattle from the little pile of toys at the end of the sofa and handed it to her. Kris took the rattle and immediately put it in her mouth.

The kitchen phone rang. Gracie picked up Kris, placed her in the playpen, and rushed to the phone.

"Hello."

"Hi, honey—what are you doing?" Billy said.

"I just changed the baby's diaper."

"Oh, fun stuff, huh?"

"Actually yes. She had a good nap, and she's happy and all giggly."

Kris still wanted to play and wasn't happy that her mother had put her in the playpen. She started to cry.

"It doesn't sound like she's happy to me," Billy said, amused.

"She wants out of the playpen."

"I'll let you go and take her out, but I wanted to ask you to find someone to stay with the girls tonight so we can go to a movie."

Gracie felt a tiny wave of excitement go through her body. "Really? Oh yes—I'll call Mom and call you back. I would love to go. I haven't been anywhere in so long," Gracie said, her excitement growing.

"We can have a date night. Is there something you want to see?" Billy said.

"No, not really. I don't care what we see. I just want to go someplace."

"Oh, and I forgot to tell you. I invited Charlie and his wife over on Saturday night for a Southern fried dinner. They're from Panama and never had Southern food, so I thought it would be something fun to do. I'll cook my mom's fried chicken and mashed potatoes. You'll make the beans and cornbread. Is that all right?" Billy asked, knowing Gracie would love the idea.

Gracie couldn't keep the excitement out of her voice. "Billy, that's more than all right—that's wonderful. We haven't had friends over since before I had the baby."

"I have to go back to work. Call me if your mom can watch the girls. Bye, see you at about five thirty," Billy said as he hung up the phone.

"Oh boy." Gracie jumped up and down, clapping her hands. The baby girl in the playpen giggled, thinking her mother was playing with her again.

"Krystal Jean, your daddy is taking me out on a date. I'm so excited. I've got to wash my hair and find something nice to wear. First, I gotta call Mom and see if she'll come over and watch you two pumpkins. Your daddy has sure been happy since he got that promotion. When your daddy is happy, your mommy is happy."

Chapter 35

Saturday, June 15, 1963

"Hello."

"Hi, Daddy, how are you?" Gracie said.

"I'm hotter than hell. How are you and the girls out there in California?"

"We're fine. I'm putting some pictures of Mary and Kris in the mail today," Gracie answered.

"Good, I'd love to come out there and see you all, but since Kodak and 3M put in those new manufacturing buildings in Garberville, I've got a lot of work going on. All those executives they brought in to run their businesses need new houses to live in, and they've hired me to do the finish work."

"That's great, Daddy. How's your back holding up?"

"Well, I'm still hobbling around, but I'm okay," he answered. "How are you and Billy doing? Is Billy still at Castle and Cook?"

"Yes, he got another promotion," Gracie said with pride in her voice.

"Well, how about that? Sounds like that boy is pretty smart."

"Yes, Daddy, he is very smart."

"How's your mother?" William asked cautiously.

"She's fine. She got a job at San Jose Hospital as a nurse's aide after she came back to California. I don't know if I was supposed to tell you that," she said.

"Gracie Lyn, I messed up big this time, and I think she left me for good."

"Yes, I think so. She won't tell me what happened, but I know she wants you to leave her alone and let her make a new life for herself."

"Yes, I know. I'm going to try. I've made a real mess of everything, and cain't get out of it," William said quietly.

Not wanting to hear what bad things her daddy did this time, she cut him off and said, "Daddy, that's not why I called you."

Having second thoughts about talking to him, she began to cry. "I'm sorry, Daddy, I probably shouldn't have called."

"Gracie Lyn, what's going on? What's wrong; tell me," William said, his voice deepening in concern.

"Daddy, I'm pregnant again, and I'm afraid to tell Billy," Gracie said sniffing loudly.

"Why, do you think he'll get mad?" he asked.

"No. Oh, I don't know, but I don't think so."

"Hell, honey, go ahead and tell him. If he gives you any grief, you tell me, and I'll have a talk with him."

"It's not that I think he'll get mad. I'm just scared. I'm worried about having another baby. Kris is only a year old. Daddy, I don't know if I can handle three babies," she said, clearly distraught.

"You can handle it, Gracie. I know you can. You're a strong girl. Talk to your mother—she'll help you," William said encouragingly.

"I know. I should talk to her. I don't know why I told you first. I just called without thinking. I'd better go. Mom will be going to work soon, and I want to call her and ask her to stop by my house. I need to tell her while I have the nerve, and before she notices my belly bump," Gracie said, trying to sound brave.

Later that day Edna pulled up in front of the little gray and white duplex and turned off the engine. Looking out the car window, she mused, "What does Gracie have to tell me this time? I hope she's not pregnant again; Krystal is still so young, and that duplex is so small. It's really too small for the four of them. How will Billy take care of them financially if she's pregnant?

Edna got out of the car. Standing on the sidewalk, looking down the street, she noticed the children playing tag on a lawn in front of one of the duplexes. A group of women sat in folding chairs nearby, talking, laughing, and enjoying the perfect sunny day.

I wonder why Gracie hasn't met any women on this block. It looks like a good place for her to meet some young mothers like herself, Edna thought as she continued down the sidewalk to Gracie's front door.

She walked into the house without knocking. "Hellooo, Gracie, are you here?"

The toddler came hurrying from the bedroom. "Granny, Granny," she cried as she wrapped her arms around Edna's leg.

Edna bent down, picked up the child, and immediately started kissing her on the cheek and neck, saying, "I'm gonna get your sugar, you good girl, I'm gonna get your sugar."

Mary twisted away squealing and laughing. "No, not my sugar!"

Gracie came from the bedroom with Kris resting high on her left hip. "You had better save some of that sugar for me," Gracie said with a smile.

"Okay, I'll give it back so there will be some for you," Edna said to Gracie as she began smooching on Mary's cheek.

Mary's squeals became louder.

Carefully putting Mary down, Edna reached for the toddler on Gracie's hip.

"Gimme that sweet baby. I need some of her sugar too," she said in a baby-talk voice.

"Okay, but you can't take all her sugar. I don't need a sour baby around here," Gracie said, laughing at the smacking sounds coming from her mother.

After a few minutes of listening to the smacking and giggling, Gracie said, "Will you cut that out—we have things to talk about."

Going into the kitchen, Gracie asked, "Mom, how would you like a cup of coffee and a piece of lemon ice-box pie?"

"Great. Am I supposed to sit down while we have this talk?" Edna asked.

"Yes, I think it would be a good idea," Gracie answered.

Edna rolled her eyes and sat Kris down on the carpet, giving her a little swat on the behind as she wobbled away on her tiny unsteady legs. "Run along, Kris—Granny has to talk to Mommy about when the new baby is due," Edna said.

Shocked, Gracie turned around quickly to see if her mother was smiling or frowning.

Chapter 36

Sunday, September 15, 1963

Walking away from the dishes soaking in the kitchen sink, Gracie went into the living room, when she heard an announcement of a news alert coming from the television. Suddenly she cried out, "Oh no!" and fell into a sitting position onto the carpet. Tears running down her cheeks, she shook her head back and forth in disbelief.

There on the TV screen was a picture of what was left of a church in Birmingham, Alabama. Someone had set off a bomb in the Sunday school area at the back, leaving much of the front still intact. Black soot surrounded the blown-out windows and front door. Wisps of smoke ascended from the roof, and a disfigured magnolia tree stood near the church with leaves crinkled and burnt from the heat. The smoldering black remains of the Sunday school rooms were scattered onto the green lawn and across the parking lot.

The newscaster, tears running down his cheeks, spoke the names of the four teenage girls that died in the blast. The whole Negro community gathered at the church parking lot while authorities, concerned that there would be a riot, called the National Guard for backup. Soon Negros and whites were in the streets with clubs, guns, and whatever fighting object they could carry. Nothing had happened yet, but it seemed to be just a matter of time.

Billy walked in through the front door and came to a dead stop.

"What's wrong, Gracie?" he said, walking quickly toward her. He bent down and touched her shoulder. "What's wrong? Tell me," he said again.

"Look," was all she managed to say, pointing at the television.

While Gracie continued to sob, Billy watched as men in white coats placed a small covered body onto a stretcher and into a waiting ambulance.

"Oh my God," he said

Gracie couldn't stop crying. Billy lifted her up and guided her to a chair at the table and she sat down. He brought her a glass of water and sat in the chair across from her.

"Come on, Gracie, we can't do anything about what's happening in Alabama. We don't live in the South anymore. Thank goodness for that, right?" he said.

"I have lived my life trying to ignore all the crap out there, and I can't anymore. What have we done bringing our kids into a world that's so horrible and scary? All the bad things that are happening in Alabama and Mississippi, the riots, and that man Medger Evers, killed by the Ku Klux Klan in front of his house with his children watching—it all makes me sick. I don't understand how people can be so stupid and mean. The good people like Martin Luther King and the peaceful demonstrators that marched in Washington really want to be peaceful, but . . ."

Billy handed her a paper napkin from the holder on the table. She took a deep breath, blew her nose, and wiped her eyes.

"Those damn KKK men killed those four little girls—I know it. I can't stand it. All my life I've had to hear people saying bad stuff about the Negros. It's wrong just wrong," Gracie ranted.

"Here—your mascara is all over your face," Billy said, handling her another napkin. "Your mom and dad never called Negros bad names."

"I know MaMaw and PaPaw never did either," she said, taking the napkin.

Wiping her cheeks and blowing her nose again, she continued her deluge of anger and fear. "I got so scared when they told us that the Russians were going to use the missiles in Cuba to bomb us. Look at all the soldiers that fought and died in the world wars, and in Korea. And look at what's happening in Vietnam. I heard that they are going to send more military advisers over there, but they're not calling it a war. Right? So many people are going to be dying. So many innocent boys will be drafted and die—because of what? I don't know. I don't understand!

"Gracie, please calm down. You can't do anything about this crazy world," Billy said sympathetically.

"Why can't there be peace? Why are people so hateful?" Gracie sobbed again.

"Mommy, Mommy" came the loud cry from the girls' bedroom.

"I'll get her," Billy said, jumping up from the table.

"Oh! Shoot," Gracie said, getting up and going to the sink and splashing water on her face.

After drying her face with a dish towel, she went into the bedroom. Billy held Mary tightly while whispering softly in her ear trying to soothe her. Seeing her mother in the doorway, Mary reached out, her little hands grabbing frantically at the air, wanting her mommy to hold her. Gracie swiftly took her in her arms and held her as tightly as she could.

"I'm sorry, baby. Mommy didn't mean to scare you. It's okay—everything is okay."

Kris stood up in her crib, her eyes open wide in fear and confusion. Billy noticed and went to the crib and picked her up, kissed her cheek, and said, "Well now, it looks like Daddy needs to make dinner tonight. How about fried chicken, gravy, black-eyed peas, and biscuits? Mommy will make a peach cobbler. Right, Mommy?"

Gracie, eyes red and face blotched from crying, held Mary tightly against her chest as she turned toward Billy and smiled. "Thank you. Sure, I'll make a cobbler."

Chapter 37

Monday, October 15, 1963
Billy's Office,
Castle and Cook, San Jose, CA

Billy laughed when he realized that he was tapping his pencil to the rhythm of "Love Me Do," a song that he normally didn't really like much. "Those Beatles do have a nice catchy sound," he said out loud.

"Who are you talking to?" came the familiar voice of a man standing in the doorway of Billy's cubicle. Startled, Billy turned and saw his friend Jake standing there.

"Jake, what are you doing here; how did you get in here?" he said, jumping up to greet him.

"I work here now—in Receiving, downstairs. I started yesterday. I remembered this was the building where you worked, so I decided to look you up on my lunch break."

"What a nice surprise. I'm on my lunch too—or I should say I was working through lunch, but now let's go down to the lunch room and get a Coke and catch up," Billy said happily.

After entering the cafeteria, they chose a table away from the cashier and the crowded area near the front.

"I'll get us a couple of Cokes from the vending machine, okay?" Billy asked.

"Sure, that'll be fine. Find an ashtray too. There isn't one on this table," Jake said.

Billy walked toward the Coke machine with Jake closely watching.

"That's sure one fine-looking man," Jake said to himself.

When Billy returned, Jake asked, "How's Gracie and the little girl doing?"

Billy set the ashtray and two Cokes on the table and said, "They're good. I have another daughter—she's a year old, and Gracie is pregnant again. We're hoping for a boy this time."

Jake looked startled for a moment and then said, "Aren't you taking this 'going straight' a little too far?"

"I told you I'm not a gay. I was mixed up and confused," Billy replied, obviously upset.

"Okay, okay, I was just teasing. How are you, my friend?" Jake asked, sincerely apologetic.

"I'm doing all right. We just moved again. We've moved six or seven times since we've been in California. I hope we don't have to do that again for a while, or that we can at least wait until the kids get too big to live in our new place. It's only two bedrooms, but it'll be just fine for quite a while."

"Listen to you, all domestic, and everything," Jake said, again sarcastically.

"Jake, I am domestic. I'm a husband and a father, and I take that very seriously."

"All right, I believe you, but let's talk about the elephant in the room—Ty. He was terribly hurt when you left and went back to Gracie. I don't think he's over you yet," Jake said as he put out the cigarette in the ashtray.

He reached into his pocket, pulled out the cigarette pack, and offered one to Billy. Billy took one and tapped the open end on the table before lighting it.

Taking a deep draw on the cigarette and blowing it out slowly, Billy said, "I don't want to talk about Ty. I don't want to know anything about him. Please, I'm not interested."

"That seems awfully cold, but, okay—if that's the way you want it," Jake said.

"That's the way I want it," Billy said.

"Let's talk about what I really came up here to talk about—Roller Derby. The Bay Area Bombers are starting next week, and I want to go. You're the only person I know that likes it. How about we go to the Derby on Wednesday night? Gracie can come too. I'd love to meet the woman that straightened you out—just kidding. I really would like to meet her."

"Gracie doesn't like to go when she is expecting. It's too nerve-wracking for her. I've been thinking about going. Give me your extension number and I'll call you on Monday and let you know," Billy said with a hint of excitement in his voice.

Friday, November 22, 1963

Billy opened the front door quietly and tiptoed into the house. All the lights were out, and everyone seemed to be asleep. He went into the bathroom and removed a bottle of mouthwash from under the sink and took a sip, swished it around, and spit it in the toilet. After removing his clothes, he took his pajamas from the hook at the back of the door and slipped them on.

He pulled down the toilet lid and sat down. Running his fingers through his hair, he buried his face in his hands. "Why did I leave work go to the bar? Jake didn't tell me that Chip and Scott were going to meet us there. One drink, just one drink—that's all I wanted. I didn't need to be with those guys. It brought back too many memories. Why did I go to that bar with them? I know better. It was a lot of fun dancing again, but getting drunk wasn't a smart thing to do. Oh shit, what's Gracie going to say about me not calling her when they announced that Kennedy was assassinated? I know she expected me to call. I just couldn't let her know where I was, and that I'd been drinking."

From the bedroom, Gracie called out, "Billy, where have you been? I can't believe you didn't come home sooner. Are you all right?"

"Yes, I'm alright, I was in the bathroom. I had to take a leak," Billy said, walking into the bedroom.

Seeing Gracie sitting on the edge of the bed fully clothed, her eyes red and puffy—obviously from hours of crying—Billy rushed to her side, "I'm sorry, I'm so sorry. I should have called as soon as I heard, but we were tied up in a conference room, and no one told us. We worked until eight, and I just found out about Kennedy."

"I can't believe it. President Kennedy is dead, Billy. Someone shot our president," Gracie sobbed.

Chapter 38

Thursday, February 27, 1964
O'Connor Hospital, San Jose, CA

Dr. Cunningham walked into the labor room and said politely, "Mr. Baxter, you can wait outside. We're going to give her a spinal block, and after a few minutes she won't feel a thing from the waist down."

Gracie looked up at Billy. He smiled, took her hand, and said, "Good, no pain this time. I'll be right outside."

Gracie watched as Billy walked across the room and out the door. Sadness engulfed her, and she began to cry softly. Dear God, please let this baby be a boy. Billy wants a boy so bad. Maybe he'll be happy again if he has a boy, Gracie prayed.

"It's okay, honey, this won't hurt. Only a little prick with the needle. You're going to love not having those labor pains," the doctor said.

Gracie looked up at her doctor, and he smiled. "I'm crying because I'm so happy," she lied.

Although she felt safe with this tall, big-boned doctor with red hair, who looked more like a farmer from Kansas than a doctor that delivered babies, she still couldn't tell him everything about her unhappy married life.

"Turn over on your left side, and I'll insert this syringe in the base of your spine. In about a half hour, you won't be able to feel your feet. We'll have to tell you when to push, so when I say 'push,' you give it all you got. You got that?"

"Yes, Dr. Cunningham," was all Gracie could manage to say

An hour after the delivery Billy got up from the waiting-room chair as the doctor approached. "It's a boy," the doctor said.

Shaking the doctor's hand vigorously, he said, "Wow, I thought for sure it would be another girl," Billy said, grinning from ear to ear. "How's Gracie?"

"She's very tired, but sleeping right now. Her blood pressure is elevated. We did a blood draw, and the test shows a high level of white blood cells, which tells us that an infection is somewhere in her body. We can't seem to pinpoint it, but we think it's a kidney infection, so we're giving her sulfa. Sulfa will work quickly, if that's the problem. Her blood pressure is abnormally high, so I requested a nurse by her bedside taking it every hour until we're sure it's normal again," Dr. Cunningham said.

Seeing the worry on the young man's face, the doctor placed his hand on Billy's shoulder and said, "She's sleeping now, and we're going to take a few more tests in a little while. You can go to the nursery, see your boy, go home, and get some rest. When Gracie wakes up, I'll tell her you'll be back in a little while. Try not to worry. We'll take good care of her."

"I'll stay for a while and wait for her to wake up. I would like to reassure her that everything is alright," Billy said.

"I'll walk with you to the nursery. When you're ready, Gracie is in Room 206," the doctor said.

Dr. Cunningham walked up to the nurses' station and asked to see Gracie's chart.

"Her blood pressure went up a little," the nurse said quietly after Billy passed the station and went into Gracie's room. "That couple looks so young," she said.

"They are young. She's twenty-two, and he's twenty-four. Can you imagine, twenty-four, and now responsible for a wife and three children. We must make sure he doesn't lose his wife," the worried doctor said.

Billy walked into his mother's house and flopped down on the sofa with a thud.

Nell came into the room, and seeing the gloom on Billy's face asked, "What's wrong, Son? Did something happen?"

Billy sighed. "Gracie's blood pressure is high, and the doctors are worried that she'll have a stroke. They gave her a medication to bring it down, but it won't go back to normal. Her doctor said there's an infection. They have a nurse with her at all times. She's sleeping, so I came here hoping to get something to eat and a little nap."

"I'm sure she is in good hands, Dr. Cunningham is the best. Is the baby okay?" she asked.

Billy's face brightened with a smile. "Yes, he's great. His head is sure pointed, and his feet are crooked. The pediatrician said that his head would go back to normal in a few days, but his feet will take some time to straighten. He seems long. They forgot to tell me what he weighed and how long he is. He's dark like Mary."

"You didn't tell me what you're going to name him," his mother said.

"William Scott!" Billy exclaimed.

"Another William?"

"Yes, I'm not naming him after William; I always thought that if I had a son his name would be William Scott, so we'll just have to call the baby Scott."

"I think that is a fine name, Billy Scott," she said, patting Billy on his arm.

"Is Esther going to bring the girls here when it's time for her to go to work?" she asked.

"Yes, she goes to work at three thirty," he answered.

"Will you be here for dinner?"

"No, I'm going back to the hospital after I sleep a little. I think I'll stay at the hospital until they can give me some information on what's wrong with Gracie. Besides, the nurse thinks it's a good idea if I feed the baby since Gracie can't. I'm looking forward to getting to know my son," Billy said happily. Leaning his head on the pillow, he closed his eyes for some much-needed sleep.

Nell, reaching for the comforter on the back of the sofa, gently placed it over Billy. Tiptoeing from the room, she whispered to herself, "I'm gonna make that boy some chicken 'n' dumplin's, maybe even a pie. I bet he'll eat if it's on the table when he wakes up."

Wednesday, March 2, 1964

Gracie looked across the hospital room and saw the short, plump nurse placing a clean towel and washcloth on the table near the sink. Gracie coughed.

The nurse turned around and said, "I'm Nancy, your nurse for today. Do you feel like holding your baby for a while after your bath? Your blood pressure is a little lower this morning, and the doctor said it will be alright."

"Yes, I was hoping I could see him today. I only had a chance to hold him once," Gracie answered eagerly.

"Alrighty now, let's get you bathed so I can bring him in, and you can hold your sweet baby boy," Nancy said as she brought a basin of water to the table beside Gracie's bed.

Chapter 39

Wednesday, March 3, 1964
Gracie and Billy's Duplex

With Edna holding Gracie's arm in an effort to help her in bed, Gracie slipped under the covers.

"Oh my gosh," she said, "it feels so good to be in my own bed after five days in the hospital. Happy birthday to me!"

"I'm sure it does, you brought home a sweet birthday present" Edna said.

"Sure did. Is the baby asleep?"

"Yes, he is. I bet he's going to be a really good baby," Edna said.

"I hope so. He's going to need to be," Gracie said.

"I'll stay until Billy comes home from work, and then I must go to work myself. I'll be back in the morning. I'm sure you can handle it tonight."

"I'm sure we can. We're getting to be old hands at this baby stuff," Gracie said, smiling to reassure her mother.

Around eleven p.m., Gracie laid the swaddled baby carefully into the bassinette and turned off the light. What a good baby, not even a whimper. He ate, burped, and went right to sleep. Thank goodness, Billy needs his sleep too, she thought.

Wanting to pee, she turned and walked toward the bathroom. As she reached the commode, a sharp searing pain in her side made her cry out. "Owwww, what is that?"

Bent over from the pain, she pulled down her panties and sat on the commode. She sat there for a few minutes and realized that the pain wasn't going to go away. She tried to pull herself up, but the pain surged through her pelvis and up her back so strongly that she fell back down. She screamed in pain.

Billy rushed into the bathroom. "Gracie, what's wrong?"

"I don't know. It hurts so bad, I can't get up."

"What hurts?"

"My bottom! I can't stand it, Billy. I can't stand it." Gracie began to cry.

"I'll call Dr. Cunningham. I'll be right back." Billy hurried out of the bathroom, visibly shaking.

Billy returned in a few minutes. "Dr. Cunningham is on his way. He's coming here."

"Thank you. Oh God, thank you."

Dr. Cunningham's imposing figure stood in the bathroom doorway looking down at Gracie sitting on the commode bent over moaning, "It hurts so much, it hurts so much."

Going to her, the doctor slipped one arm under her legs and the other around her back and lifted the whimpering young woman into his arms. He carried her out of the bathroom and laid her on her bed.

With soothing remarks and explanations, the doctor examined Gracie. Soon he went to his physician's bag, took out a syringe, and carefully injected something into her behind. Within seconds, Gracie stopped moaning.

Looking up at the doctor with red swollen eyes, Gracie said, "Thank you, Doctor Cunningham, thank you so much. Do you know what's wrong?"

"Not yet. Come into my office tomorrow morning at eleven, and we'll find out what this is all about. This injection should keep the pain away for about six hours. You go to sleep now and don't get up with the baby. Let Billy handle it, alright?"

Gracie nodded her head.

"Billy, let's go in the living room," the doctor said.

"Do you know what's wrong?" Billy asked once there.

"No, I'm not sure, but I have some ideas. I called El Camino Hospital, and they have no available rooms. I want you to bring her to my office tomorrow morning at eleven, and I'll do a proper exam. I'll leave you some pain medication, and you can give her some every four hours when the injection wears off." Patting Billy on the shoulder, the doctor said, "Try not to worry."

Thursday, March 4, 1964
Dr. Cunningham's Office,
Santa Clara, CA

The doctor gave Gracie an injection after the exam, and now she was sleeping on the exam table while Billy dozed in the chair at her bedside.

Dr. Cunningham walked into the room. "Hello, you two," he said quietly, trying not to startle them.

They opened their eyes and said hello simultaneously.

"Billy may I speak with you in the hall? Gracie needs to sleep," the doctor asked.

Leading Billy out of the room, the doctor started his explanation right away. "It seems that the complete lining of Gracie's uterus has a serious bacterial infection. I'd like her to go to the hospital, but there are no rooms available. So Gracie is to go to bed and stay there with no activity whatsoever; she can only get up to go to the bathroom. I'll give her a prescription of morphine for the pain, and I'll come by every evening at eight to give her a shot to fight the infection. She'll probably sleep most of the time with the pain medication, and it will probably take a week to ten days before this infection heals. You'll need to have someone take the girls out of the house and perhaps someone to look after the baby and Gracie during the day. Can you find someone to help you out?"

"Yes," Billy said.

Dr. Cunningham walked to the exam room door then turned and faced Gracie before opening it. "This sure is a hell of a way to spend your birthday, but don't worry I'll see to it that you get well quickly so you can celebrate later."

Gracie smiled and simply said, "Thank you for everything."

Dr. Cunningham stood at the nursing station counter writing instructions into Gracie's chart, when his nurse approached. "Doctor, I overheard what you said to Gracie Baxter about no room at the hospital. There may be a room after all. Mrs. Thompson is not going to be admitted today."

"I know, Janet, but this young couple has three children, and they really can't afford a hospital bill. Their place is on my way home, so I'll stop by after my hospital rounds and save them the expense."

Janet watched as the doctor walked away and stopped at the door to the exam room where his next patient waited. "We work for a wonderful doctor," she said to the approaching nurse.

The nurse gave her a quizzical look.

"Doctor Cunningham knows the young woman in Room 5 needs to go to the hospital but thinks the couple can't afford it, so he's going to do a house call every evening on his way home."

"You're kidding, right?" said the nurse.

"Nope. He just told me. What a man," Nurse Janet said with a sigh.

Chapter 40

Monday, March 16, 1964

Billy sat at his desk sorting papers and placing them
into individual manila file folders as Jake entered his office.

Knocking on the door frame, he asked,"Hello, working
hard?, ? Want to go to lunch?"

Turning and looking in Jake's direction, "Sure, I could
use a break. Meet me downstairs in about five minutes. I need
to call Gracie, and then I'll come down. Billy ansered.

Entering the break room, Billy found Jake sitting at
their usual table near the Coke machine. He set his bag lunch
on the table and carefully removed the sandwich and napkin.

"Little wife making your lunch again, I see," Jake said
sarcastically.

"Yes, she's well, as far as I can tell. She still has some
residual pains from the sloughing off of the dead skin in her
uterus, but that shouldn't last long," Billy said with
confidence.

"Ugh, don't talk about that while I'm trying to eat my
soup," Jake said, making a disgusting face.

Billy laughed. "If I have to know about this stuff, you,
as my friend, must know about it too."

"Okay, okay, I'll change the subject. Now that Gracie is better, can we go out for a drink?"

"Is there still a Roller Derby match this month? If so, I'll tell Gracie that's where I'm going," Billy said.

"There's a match next Thursday. It's a yes then?"

"Yes, I really do need a break," Billy said, rolling his eyes.

"The bar after?" Jake asked.

"Maybe for one drink. Our son has an appointment tomorrow with the orthopedic doctor. He has inverted ankles. It's time to put the casts on his legs. He'll have them on for about a year. They told us he would be okay," Billy said with feigned confidence.

"Shit, more problems for you. I'm so glad I'll never get married and have kids. It seems to me that all they do is create stress and problems. You're only twenty-three, right? How do you manage to keep your sanity?" Jake said asked, shaking his head.

"You keep it because you have to. They depend on me, and I love them," Billy said.

Monday, September 21, 1964

On her knees with her head down, her mind fully occupied with planting flowers in her new flowerbed, Gracie didn't see the two women walking toward her until they were standing two feet from her busy hands. Gracie looked up and jumped when she saw the two unfamiliar faces staring down at her.

"Hi, I'm Carla; this is Helen. I live on the other side of the next duplex, and Helen lives three down," said the young woman with short blond hair.

Gracie's face turned red in response to the shyness she felt. "Hi, I'm Gracie."

"We've seen you coming and going with your children, and we wanted to introduce ourselves. There are mostly families with kids on this block," Helen said.

"You have two little girls don't you?" Carla asked.

"Yes, and a baby boy. He's almost seven months old."

"Oh, I didn't know. Congratulations. I have a two-year-old girl and a five-year-old boy. Helen has a two-year-old girl. We have a babysitting co-op on this block, and we thought you might want to join. We take turns watching each other's children, and there's no money involved. We keep track by logging the hours."

"That sounds interesting. How does it work?"

"If you babysit for two hours for me, that means I owe you two hours of babysitting. I'm the secretary and keep track of everyone's hours. Of course, you also should keep track so we can always compare."

"I'll have to talk to my husband and see what he thinks about it," Gracie said.

"That's fine. Talk to him and come on down to my house and let me know. Some of the wives meet at my house at about eleven every day, or when the kids go down for a nap. Come over and have a cup of coffee. Your kids can play with our kids. There's always a pot of coffee on the stove," the friendly, smiling Carla said reassuringly.

Monday, December 14, 1964

The baby boy sat in the wooden high chair pounding with his hands as Gracie put a small amount of ground peas and carrots from the baby food grinder up to his mouth.

"Come on, Scottie, let's finish these good vegetables. One more bite," she said, coaxing him with a little tap to his lips.

Looking out the patio door, Gracie could see her two little girls bundled in their puffy coats, playing happily on this exceptionally warm winter day. Mary sat at a little table pouring pretend tea into a tiny cup and saucer. Kris happily pushed her play horse back and forth across the patio.

"I gotta get you fed so Daddy can have his dinner when he gets home," she said more to herself than to the baby in front of her.

Grabbing the spoon from her hand, the giggling baby banged it on the high chair tray. Smooshed peas and carrots flew everywhere. Taking a napkin from the table, Gracie wiped his face and hands, unlatched the tray from the high chair, and picked him up. "Okay, you're done, big boy!"

She walked to the patio door, then opened it and called to the little girls, "Come on in and get your hands and face washed. Your daddy should be home in a few minutes."

Setting Scottie in the playpen, she gave him a rattle and several bright-colored toys to keep him busy while she put dinner on the table. Billy liked to eat dinner as soon as he arrived home from work at five thirty, and Gracie liked to accommodate him.

After dinner, Billy turned to Gracie. "Have you finished putting the kids to bed? There are some things we need to talk about," he said.

"Yes, they're in bed, and boy, I'm sure ready to sit down now," Gracie said as she pulled out a dining room chair and sat across from Billy.

Getting to the point right away, Billy said, "I enjoyed meeting everyone at the block meeting last night."

"I'm glad you're finally getting a chance to meet our neighbors. Who was at the meeting?" Gracie asked.

"Carla's husband, Dick; Linda's husband, Johnny; John from next door; Lou from four doors down; and Sheri," Billy answered.

"Sheri? I thought this was a meeting for the husbands to plan our block Christmas party," Gracie said.

"Sheri isn't married, and she wanted to have a say about what we were planning, so we let her stay. It was a good meeting, but I wanted to talk to you about something else. After the meeting Dick was laughing about how all you women spend most of your day at Carla's house drinking coffee and gossiping. Do you really do that?" Billy asked, sounding annoyed.

"Well, yes, I go over to her house for a little while every day, but I don't spend all day, and we don't gossip. We just have coffee, talk, laugh, and sometimes listen to the news. It's fun. I like talking to Carla. She's very nice and becoming a really good friend."

"What do you do with the kids?" Billy asked.

"We bring the kids to her house and let them play together. Sometimes, when they take a nap, I run over there for a minute or two, but not for long."

"What do you do besides talk?" Billy asked.

"We make lunch together, we talk about the news, we do our mending, and sometimes we even bring our ironing boards and iron together. It's nice to have friends, Billy," Gracie said pleadingly, fearing that Billy was going to tell her not to go anymore. "I still do all my work, and everything is the same as before I met Carla. The house is clean, dinner is on time, the kids are clean and fed."

"I'm not going to tell you not to go, just don't gossip too much, and don't tell them too much about what happened . . . before," Billy said.

"Oh, Billy, I would never do that. You know I wouldn't."

"Alright, and make a dessert for Friday. I want to invite the new couple next door over for cards," Billy said.

"Every time I sit at the table, one of them looks through the kitchen windows at me and smiles. I like the sun coming in that window or I would keep it closed," Gracie said. "What are their names?" she asked.

"John and Sharon. No need for closing the window—they're nice and friendly. I talked to them when I was mowing the lawn yesterday. She works at Bank of America downtown; he's going to San Jose State."

"Alright, I'll make a cake tomorrow," Gracie said, relieved at the change of subject. All Billy seemed to be worried about was if she told Carla about his past.

"You know Bud and Joy are supposed to come over Friday and play cards with us," Gracie said

"I forgot. I guess you'll be making two desserts then," Billy said with a smile.

"Yes, I guess I will," Gracie said, smiling back at him.

Chapter 41

Tuesday, December 22, 1964
Tinkers Damn Bar
San Jose, CA

The three men at the bar watched the men on the dance floor through the mirror on the back wall of the bar.

"Do you want to dance?" Jake asked Billy.

"No, I need to leave. I need to go to Sears," Billy said. "I told Gracie I was going Christmas shopping, and I need to bring home some gifts. Do you want to go with me?"

Downing the drink in his hand, Jake said sarcastically, "No, I really don't feel like being that domestic. Watching you buy the little wife and kids a present doesn't interest me. I'll let you do your husband duties alone."

"Leave him alone," said Tom, the handsome blond sitting at Billy's left. "You're always picking on him."

"I don't pick on Billy. I'm just teasing. He knows that. Right, Billy?" Jake said.

"Not always. Sometimes I take you seriously," Billy answered.

"Don't be silly. It's a game we play. You play a straight man that likes to have queer friends, and I play like I don't believe you are straight," Jake said, smiling.

"I don't play games. I have three kids at home. Gracie and the kids need me. I love them. I go out with you because I think you're my friend, and for a break in my routine. I wish you would just be my friend and understand."

"Sorry, I didn't know you were so keyed up about it. I'm going to go now. I'll let you two go to Sears and buy gifts," Jake said as he got up from the bar stool.

"See you at work," Billy said.

"See you at lunch," Jake answered.

Billy watched the reflection of the men dancing and longed to go onto the dance floor and let off some steam. He missed dancing in the worst way. The rhythmic sound of this disco music stirred something in him more than any music he had heard in a long time.

Taking a deep breath and then a sigh, he asked the blond young man, "Do you want to go to Sears with me, Tom?"

"Sure, I love to shop, and I also need to buy my mom a Christmas gift. I don't have a car here. Can you give me a lift home after shopping?" Tom asked.

"Where do you live?" Billy asked.

"On Moorpark, near Bascom," Tom said.

"I can drop you off. I live near Stokes Street," Billy said.

"Great, we're practically neighbors," Tom said with a wide smile.

A flash of unwanted memories of Ty sent a shiver down Billy's spine. He turned and looked into the blue eyes of the man with the big smile and thought, Oh, no, I'm not going there again.

Saturday, March 6, 1965
Brass Rail Dance Club,
San Jose, CA

The three couples in the gray Plymouth could hear the thumping of the loud music coming from the Brass Rail Bar and Strip Club as the car circled around and around the parking lot while trying to find a place to park.

'There's one over there at the back; over there, Billy, over there," Gracie said, her voice shrill with excitement.

"Okay, okay, I see it," Billy said.

"Haven't you been to a strip club before?" Bud asked.

"No, and I've only been to a bar a couple of times. We went to see the Righteous Brothers at the Saddle Rack a couple of years ago. Oh yeah, and we were at a bar in Tahoe once. It was a restaurant too, so I could get in. I hope I don't have a problem getting in. I don't have a driver's license. I brought my birth certificate," Gracie said.

"They check IDs carefully here, and they may not let you in with a birth certificate," John said.

"How do you know?" Sharon asked suspiciously.

"Remember, I went with some guys from school. I told you about that," John said.

Sharon thought for a minute and said, "Oh, yes, I remember."

"Have you been here before, Bud?" Joy asked.

"Yes, a long time ago before we were married," Bud said.

Standing in the doorway with the bouncer checking everyone's driver's license, Gracie carefully unfolded her birth certificate. When her turn came, she looked up, smiled innocently, and handed the document to him. Scanning the paper with his flashlight, he said, "I can't accept this. You must have a driver's license or an ID card."

"What? That's legal. Did you look at the date? I'm twenty-three years old. I have three kids. There's nothing in that room that I haven't seen before," Gracie said, her voice getting higher with each word.

"Sorry, honey—no ID, no getting in here," the big bruiser said, looking down at Gracie with almost a grin.

"Oh come on, it's her birthday," Bud said to the bouncer.

"Can't do it; it's the law. Do any of you want to come in?" the big man asked.

"No, we all came together. I'm sorry, guys. Do you have any suggestions where we can go now?" Billy asked.

"Gracie said she wanted to do something wild and crazy, and this was the only thing I could think of," Bud said.

"Let's get a bottle of rum and go back to our place and have a party there," John suggested.

Obviously disappointed, Gracie said, "All right, that's a good idea."

Later that night:

Gracie said, "Billy, I need to get my driver's license. Mom can't keep taking me and the kids to doctor appointments all the time, and I could even go to the grocery store when I need to and not have to wait until you can take me."

"I don't think you need to get one. We only have one car ,and if you need to go someplace, I can always take you," Billy said.

"But, Billy, that's not fair. I'm stuck here with no way to go anywhere or do anything. All the other women on the block have their license."

"I don't care what all the other women have. Now let's go to bed and forget about it," Billy said.

Monday, June 28, 1965
Carla's Duplex

With Scottie snug on her hip, Gracie marveled at the sweetness of Mary holding Kris's hand as they made their way down the sidewalk to Carla's duplex.

"Knock on the door," Gracie coached the little girls when they arrived.

With two tiny knocks, the door swung open.

"Hello there, come on in," Carla said with a big welcoming smile. "Kids are in the backyard; Helen went home for some sugar for her coffee. I'm out of sugar, but you're welcome to have some of that old morning coffee. The new coffeepot kept it warm."

"Thanks," Gracie said as she came into the living room and placed Scottie on the floor. As hard as it was to move his little body across the carpet with his leg braces and separation bar, he quickly scooted himself toward the sliding glass door that led to the backyard.

"No, no, sweetheart—you can't go out there," Gracie said, picking him up. "I know you want to go out and play with the other kids." Holding him close while he whimpered in disappointment, she brought him with her to the table and sat down.

Carla reached into the cabinet and brought out a box of teething cookies, "These are the only cookies I have in the house right now," she said, handing one to the toddler.

"Thanks, Car," Gracie said.

"Do you still want to get your driver's license?" Carla said.

"You bet. I've decided I'm going to do it no matter what. I don't care if it makes Billy mad or not. My mother can't keep taking me places. She has her own life."

"I read that Del Mar High School's summer school program is offering a Driver's Ed class at night starting in September. I think it would help you get your confidence back," Carla said.

"I don't know if Billy would allow me to do that," Gracie said.

"How long has it been? Do you have any idea why he doesn't want you to drive?" Carla asked.

"It's been five years. We took the bus everywhere the first year, and after we got a car, Billy said I didn't need to get my license, that he would take me where I needed to go."

"Gracie, you have three kids, and you need a car. What happens if your mother or Billy can't take you where you need to go?" Carla asked.

"I don't know why he doesn't want me to drive; I never asked. You're right, Car, that class is a good idea. I don't think Billy will take me to the school. Shoot, I'll walk to the school if I have to!"

"It's not that far, and if he won't take you to the DMV for your driver's test, I'll take you," Carla said.

"You would do that?"

"Sure, I'll take you," Carla said with a smile.

"Thanks, Car, I'll call the school tomorrow and see what I have to do to sign up. I'm not even going to tell him until the class starts," Gracie said.

Carla reached across the table and laid a hand on Gracie's arm gently and asked, "What was going on yesterday when I came over and you were smoking Marlboros one after the other and dropping the butts on the ground? You and Billy smoke Winstons."

"Oh, I was doing something stupid. I thought if I left some cigarette butts around the yard, Billy would see them and think there was another man here with me. It was my way of trying to make him jealous. He's been so cold and distant lately. Isn't it sad that I get so desperate for his attention that I do stupid things like that?"

"Yes, it's sad. I know he cares about you. What do you think is going on with him?" Carla asked.

"I don't know. He gets in moods sometimes, and he becomes very distant," Gracie said, lying to Carla. She knew very well what the problem could be.

"It's so hard to believe. He is the fun guy of the neighborhood when he's with us, but I've seen him get moody. When he's in the house with you and the kids, he becomes very quiet and reserved," Carla said.

"I hate feeling so insecure," Gracie said, feeling her throat tighten and her eyes fill with tears.

"Are you still interested in going to the Laundromat with Linda, Sue, and me? We go every Sunday. I must tell you there's a bar, The Till Morning Lounge, next door. We go in and have a drink while we wait for our clothes to wash and dry," Carla said.

"What? Does Dick know?" Gracie said.

"I think so, but he doesn't care. Tell Billy you're going with us. You don't have to tell him about the bar part," Carla said.

"Okay, I will! I better go check on the kids. They're being very quiet. No telling what kind of trouble they're getting into," Gracie said, not wanting to talk about Billy anymore.

"Oh, they're fine. If you don't hear any crying, you can bet they're fine," Carla said, laughing.

Chapter 42

Friday, August 20, 1965
California Bistro,
San Francisco, CA

The trio walked into the little restaurant tucked in between the large retail shops and stood before the sign that said "Wait to be seated." A tall, sleek young blond man approached. "Three?" he asked.

"Yes," Jake answered.

"Follow me," the young man said.

"Anytime."

The young man turned around and smiled. "I heard that."

Jake smiled back.

The three men sat down and picked up their menus.

"I feel so devilish skipping work today," Tom said.

"I feel relieved that I'm out of that cubical and in the best city in the world," Jake said.

Billy sat quietly.

"Billy, why are you so quiet? Where's that fun guy I brought to the city with me?" Jake asked.

"I'm feeling a little guilty about lying to my boss, and I'm worried that Gracie will call the office. I told her that I would be locked up in meetings all day, but she may forget. I could get into all kinds of trouble."

"Oh, will the little wife ground you if she finds out you played hooky?" Jake joked.

"Don't start, Jake. It's my boss I'm worried about."

"Okay, okay, let's order a drink and worry only about having a fun day away from the humdrum of our daily lives. Let's eat lunch and go find us a Glory Hole," Jake said, smiling at Billy.

"Jake! Will you stop teasing me, please? I told you that I'm not going to a Glory Hole. I can go to the park and wait for you if want to go. If you thought you would talk me into it after I came up here with you, you're wrong," Billy said, frustrated with his friend.

"Stop it, Billy. We're here together, and I don't want to go either. There's an afternoon show at Club Fugazzi. Let's see if we can get in, okay?"

"Yes, I would like that and maybe the Back Stage bar. I always liked that place," Billy said.

"I guess so. You were always the diva everyone wanted to dance with," Jake said.

"Yeah, it sure helps being so handsome," Tom said as he winked at Billy.

Tom and Jake laughed loudly. Billy blushed.

The waiter walked up, smiling at the men. "You're a happy bunch. Can I take your order now?"

"Sure, and you can join us if you want," Jake offered.

"I finish work in an hour, and I'm free for the rest of the evening. I may take you up on that offer," the waiter replied.

"Okay, we could use a local fourth to make this day even more interesting," Tom said.

Sunday, August 22, 1965
Till Morning Bar and Grill,

The three women giggled and laughed as they stuffed their clothes into the Laundromat washing machines. Gracie filled the last machine with clothes and shut the door with a loud bang.

"There! All done. Let's go next door. I'm ready!" she said.

"Wow, how many loads did you have today? Carla asked.

"Ten. That's not many. I usually have more. Now Billy is talking about getting me a washing machine. I don't think he liked it when I told him that it didn't matter what he said, that I was going with you guys to do my laundry."

"That's funny. See, show him you can think for yourself, and he'll respect you more. Come on, girl, you deserve a rum and Coke for having some balls," Carla said.

Giggling, Gracie turned to Carla and said, "I can't believe you just said that."

Carla smiled and shrugged her shoulders.

The three women sat on bar stools while trying to have a conversation in spite of the music blasting from the jukebox. Four hot and sweaty men dressed in baseball uniforms came into the bar and sat at a table in the corner of the room.

The bartender yelled, "What can I get you guys?"

"We'll have a round of Budweiser," one of the men shouted back.

One by one, the women got up from the bar and walked toward the door.

"Where are you going, ladies? We were just thinking about putting a slow song on that jukebox and seeing if you wanted to have a little dance," one of the baseball-uniform-clad men shouted from across the room.

"We'll be back. We're doing our laundry next door, and we have to check on it," Carla shouted back, closing the door behind her.

Giggling like schoolgirls, the women rushed into the Laundromat.

The soothing music of "Moon River" filled the room while the three couples awkwardly danced in the gloomy bar. When the music stopped, Carla announced, "Good time's over, boys. I'm sure our clothes are dry by now. If we're too late, our husbands will be wondering where we are and come looking for us." The men laughed nervously.

As the women opened the door to go out, the one called Buster said, "Yeah, we've got the same problem at home. You girls going to be here next Saturday?"

Being the last one out the door, Linda called out, "Yeah, a girl has to do her laundry, right?"

From the front seat Carla asked Gracie, "Did I see you give that Jim guy your phone number?"

"Yes, we were having a nice conversation about his wife and their problems. He said I was easy to talk to, and he needed help understanding women. He wanted to talk to me some more about it, so I said sure and gave him my number."

Roars of laughter came from the front seat. "Oh, Gracie, you can't possibly be that naive," Carla said.

"What? What do you mean, naïve?" Gracie replied.

Friday, September 17, 1965

While the kids were taking a nap, Gracie added the final touch to making the little duplex apartment cheerful and ready for Billy to come home and receive the news. She straightened the yellow tablecloth on the kitchen table and set the bouquet of daisies in the center. She sighed and walked into the kitchen. "I hope he'll notice how much I cleaned today and be happy."

She opened the curtain on the window over the sink and looked out across the street at the little ranch-style house on the corner.

I love that house and its huge front lawn. Maybe we'll be able to afford a house like that someday, she thought.

She turned toward the cabinet and pulled out the things she needed to make cookies and said, "I think I'll make chocolate cookies while the kids are sleeping. I want everything to be perfect when I tell Billy the news. I'm not sure why I'm so excited, but it feels so good and so right."

When the phone rang, Gracie picked it up quickly so as to not wake the sleeping children. "Hello," she said brightly.

"Gracie Baxter?" questioned a male voice on the other end on the line.

"Yes, I'm Gracie," she answered.

"Jim, from Till Morning," he said.

"Oh, hi, Jim—it's so good to hear from you. I didn't think you were going to call."

"I had to think about it for a while, I wasn't sure you meant it. What are you doing this afternoon? I thought I might come by and see you."

"Oh, Jim any other day would be better. I just got a phone call from my doctor and I'm pregnant again. I'm making cookies for my husband to surprise him," she said. "Why don't you call me next week and we can talk. I hope everything is going well with you," Gracie said.

"Everything is not fine, but I gotta go. I won't call you again," Jim said, and hung up abruptly.

Gracie pulled the phone away from her ear and looked at it in disbelief. "Huh? I wonder what that was about."

Chapter 43

Wednesday, September 22, 1965

Billy had just reached his car in the parking lot, when he heard someone call his name. He turned and was surprised to see Tom waving at him from the bus stop on the corner. Billy waved for him to come over to the car.

"I was downtown and thought I would come by your office and say hello. I thought you got off work at five," Tom said.

"Normally it is five, but I wanted to go to Sears this afternoon, so I took off work a little early."

"Oh, I won't keep you. The bus should be coming by soon."

"No, why don't I give you a lift home? I won't be in Sears long. I'm going to buy Gracie a washing machine. I've already decided which one I want to buy. I just have to go in and pay for it," Billy said.

"A washing machine? Is it her birthday or something?" Tom teased.

Billy laughed. "No, she's pregnant again, and I think she needs one. It will make her happy."

Tom stared at Billy for a moment, unable to speak; his face suddenly bright red.

"What's wrong?" Billy asked, surprised at his friend's reaction.

"Nothing, nothing, I'm surprised, that's all," Tom said.

"You want to go shopping with me again? This is becoming a habit, running into each other and then going shopping," Billy said.

"Uh, what? Uh, oh yeah, running into each other. Yeah, but it's always fun," Tom stammered, still overwhelmed by Billy's news.

Two hours later, as they sat in the car out in front of Tom's apartment complex, Billy said, "You're still acting strange, Tom. Do you want to get some coffee and talk?"

"No, I'll just go home," Tom said.

"Tom, tell me what's wrong?"

Spinning around to face Billy Tom said angrily, "You want to know what's wrong. I'll tell you what's wrong! You hang out with Jake and me, you go to the city, you go to gay bars, and you act gay when you're with us, but then you keep having kids as if you're straight. Just when I think I have you figured out, you change on me. I'm in love with you, deeply and passionately! I don't approach you because you tell me you're not gay and you don't fool around. In my heart I feel that you are gay. I watch and I wait. I want to be there when you figure this out. I'm a patient man, and you're worth the wait, but all you do is keep having kids. What are you thinking? You are a gay man, Billy—you'll have to admit it someday, and I want to be there."

Billy began to sweat. Dark stains appeared on his shirt under his armpits. He looked stunned and then said, "Tom, I'm sorry. I didn't know. What can I say? I'm so damn sick of trying to explain myself to you and Jake! All my kids have been a happy accident. I'm not sorry—I love them, and I want to be a father to them. It's hard. Accidents happen. After our trip to San Francisco, I went to a smoker party and watched porn for hours with the guys on the block and then I went home to Grace. She got pregnant. This seems to be our lot in life is to have kids, because they've all been accidents. Well, except for the second daughter. I wanted to have another baby. I guess I wanted to assure myself and Gracie that I wanted to be a father and that I wasn't gay.

"Gracie and I have a perplexing relationship. She's very naive and doesn't initiate anything, and isn't sexy at all. She's a little girl in an adult woman's body, and all she wants to do is please me. I love her very much, but I am not attracted to her. I don't know how to explain it. She's started taking some self-awareness classes, and I'm sure they'll help. I want this to work, but it gets harder and harder. I think another child will help. I really do. I want a boy; two girls and two boys, the perfect family," Billy said, his voice shaky.

"It sounds to me like you don't really believe all that shit! You are a gay man, Billy, and the sooner you stop this pretending, the sooner you will be happy," Tom said, opening the car door and slamming it shut after he got out.

Billy yelled out the window, "Tom, I'm sorry. You're wrong."

Billy drove to his apartment and cut the engine. He sat in the duplex driveway, his hands still shaking from his encounter with Tom. Not wanting Gracie to see him upset, he stayed in the car and listened to the sounds coming from the house. He smiled. The sound of a cartoon show on the TV, the sound of dinner preparations going on in the kitchen, the sound of a child's laughter—all the sounds of his life in the little gray duplex where his family waited for him to come home.

"I have a good life here. Hard, and sometimes frustrating, but a good life. Tom is wrong. This is where I belong," Billy said. He got out of his car, walked to the plain gray door of his home, and opened it.

"Daddy, Daddy," came the happy cries of the children inside.

Chapter 44

Sunday, December 5, 1965

  Gracie stood on a chair and removed the boxes of Christmas ornaments from the closet shelf in the bedroom. "Billy, did you remember to buy the tinsel for the tree today?" she asked.

  "Yes, I bought four boxes. Do you think that's enough?"

  Laughing, Gracie said, "Holy cow, Billy, we'll be up to midnight putting tinsel on our tree. Maybe you'll let me fling it on this year."

  "No flinging, one tinsel at a time," Billy insisted.

  "We sure picked out a pretty Christmas tree this year. I'm glad you decided on the blue spruce. Should I wake the kids up from their nap to help us?" Gracie asked.

  "Let's go ahead and decorate it and let it be a surprise."

  "Okay," Gracie said.

  A little while later, Gracie threw a handful of tinsel at the tree and walked away. "I'm done. You and your perfect tinsel—I'm not doing this anymore. You can put the rest on one at a time. I'm through," Gracie said, smiling.

"Aw, come on. Doesn't it look nice this way?. When we put it on one strand at a time, the tinsel looks like icicles, right?" Billy grinned.

The door to the kids' bedroom opened, and Mary came out rubbing her eyes.

"Hi, sweetheart," Gracie said. "Look—Mommy and Daddy put up the Christmas tree. You can help us decorate" Gracie took Mary's hand.

As soon as Mary saw the tree, she began to jump up and down, clapping her hands. "Yay! Yay!"

Kris came into the room, walked past the brightly lit tree, and crawled into her daddy's lap.

"Look, Kris, a Christmas tree," Billy said as Kris laid her head on Billy's chest and cautiously looked toward the tree.

Whimpering sounds came from the bedroom. "I'll get him," Gracie said, leaving the room.

A minute or two after, Gracie walked out of the bedroom with their baby boy in her arms.

"Hey, Scottie, look at the Christmas tree," Billy called to his son.

Seeing all the colored lights, Scottie's baby arms reached out toward the tree.

Gracie looked at Billy and smiled. Billy winked and smiled back. "I think this is going to be a great Christmas."

Chapter 45

Friday, May 20, 1966

Gracie scooted her big belly carefully under the steering wheel, shut the car door, stuck the key in the ignition, and started the car. She took a deep breath to calm herself. Carla opened the passenger side door and got in. "Well, this is your third try. If you don't make it this time, the DMV makes you wait a year before you can try again."

"I know. It's not my driving; I can't parallel park," Gracie said.

"Maybe you need glasses? Maybe you have a stigmatism that could prevent you from being able to park." Carla said.

"You may be right, but it's too late now. I'm going to try one more time."

The DMV examiner, clipboard in hand, opened the door and slid into the car seat. He turned and looked at Gracie. His eyes opened wide in amazement.

Gracie saw the way he looked at her and thought, I bet he is saying how in hell did she get her big belly under the steering wheel?

"How far along are you Mrs. . . . ?" He looked down at his clipboard ". . . Baxter?"

"I'm nine months."

"This is the third time I've driven with you, Mrs. Baxter. You do well every time. Now let's see if you can park, so I can approve your license before you have this baby in the car," the patient DMV examiner said with a grin.

Gracie backed into the designated spot and hit the curb, backed up and tried again, and hit the curb—but this time she went over it. Her third attempt, and she'd failed again.

She covered her face with her hands to hide the tears filling her eyes. "I'm sorry. Maybe I need glasses or something. I've tried so hard to park, and I just can't do it. I'm going to have my fourth child, and I need my license so badly. I need to be able to drive."

"Fourth child?" He glanced down at his clipboard. "Oh my God, you're only twenty-four!"

Gracie bowed her head and asked, "Is it true that I must wait a year to try again?"

"Tell you what, young lady. If you promise me you won't try to parallel park until you get some glasses, I'll approve you for a license."

She jerked her head up and looked in his direction. "I promise, oh I promise."

He smiled and handed her the clipboard. "Sign and date at the bottom and take it into the building. You'll get a temporary license, and in about a month a new one will come in the mail. Oh, and good luck, sweetheart."

Gracie noticed that Carla was watching from across the parking and saw her failure to park. When the DMV person got out of the car and walked toward the DMV offices, Gracie started her car and drove it right up in front of Carla. Waving a piece of paper she screamed, "I got it, I got it. I can drive!"

That evening, the children were fed and playing in their room. On the counter sat a German chocolate cake, chicken and dumplings, black-eyed peas, fried potatoes, and cornbread kept warm and ready for Billy as soon as he walked in the door. Gracie sat at the table rubbing her swollen belly wondering what he was going to say when she told him she had passed her driver's test today.

Billy walked in the door, took one look at Gracie, and asked, "What's up? What's wrong?"

"Nothing's wrong; everything is right. I made your favorite dinner, and a German chocolate cake. The kids are fed so you can have a quiet dinner, and, oh yeah, as of today I have my driver's license."

Startled, Billy stared at her. "What? What do you mean? How?" he stammered.

"Carla took me today to the DMV, and I passed the test. We need to talk about me driving the car," Gracie said as she filled a plate with the food.

"Okay, I knew this would happen sooner or later, so I've already thought about it. You can take the car grocery shopping, and you can use it to go to the doctor, but that's all for now."

"I don't understand why, but for now that will be okay, except I want to take it when I go to Aunt Val's for my psycho-cybernetics group, and, oh yeah, I'm starting a new role-playing group at Aunt Val's. I'll need it then too."

Billy, surprised at her determined attitude, said, "Okay, that sounds reasonable, but you need to tell me what you do in these groups."

Gracie didn't let it show, but she was bubbling up inside with excitement. She filled her plate with food and calmly sat across from Billy and asked him about his day.

Chapter 46

Sunday, June 12, 1966, 6:00 a.m.

Holding a towel between her legs, Gracie dialed the phone quickly.

"Hello," Carla answered.

"Car, my water broke—can you help me?"

"Sure, where's Billy?"

"He's in the bathroom. I think he's taking a shower and shaving."

"What? I'll be right down."

Soon, Carla came barging in the front door. "How far apart are your pains?"

Gracie, sitting in a kitchen chair, holding her clean clothes in her arms, said pitifully, "They're still about fifteen minutes apart. I need to change my clothes. Can you help me?"

"Sure, here, give me those clothes."

Gracie winced in pain as the contractions started to build.

"That was only ten minutes," Carla said, jumping up from the chair she was sitting in. She went to the bathroom door. "Billy Baxter, Gracie needs to go to the hospital right now. Her pains are getting closer together."

"Carla, we've been through this before. It takes Gracie hours to deliver. There really isn't any hurry."

"If you don't come out of that bathroom right now I'm going to come in there and kick your butt, and then take your wife to the hospital."

Billy came out of the bathroom smiling. "Okay, I'll take her. I sure don't want my butt kicked."

"Billy, her water broke, and the pains are ten minutes apart. This is her fourth baby. This could be totally different delivery."

Billy opened the front door and looked at the women. "Okay, I hear you. Gracie, I'm sorry I didn't hear you say your water broke. Let's get going."

Wednesday, August 10, 1966

Edna knocked on the door a couple of times and entered the duplex, calling, "Gracie, are you here?"

Gracie, busy folding diapers in the bedroom, called back, "I'm in the kids' room."

"Sure a lot of kids sleeping in this room," Edna said, looking around at the bunk beds, single bed, and crib crowded in the room.

"I know, but I really think they like it. They keep each other company."

"Is the baby sleeping in the crib?" Edna asked.

"No, he still sleeps in the bassinet in our room, or with me most of the times. It's easier when he wakes up to nurse," Gracie said.

"How is that going?" Edna asked.

"It's great—so easy. It makes me mad that all the doctors told me not to breast-feed and that it was healthier to give the baby formula. It's crazy that they think formula is better than mother's milk. Besides, do you have any idea how many aluminum bottle sterilizers I melted when one of the kids distracted me and I forgot that it was on the stove? At least the Kaiser doctors didn't argue with me when I insisted on breast-feeding Tommy. He is such a sweet baby and so good. He laughs all the time." Gracie said.

"Where are the kids?" Edna asked.

"They're playing in the backyard."

The women went into the kitchen. Edna sat at the table. "Would you like a glass of tea? Oh yes, and I have a lemon ice-box pie in the freezer—would you like a piece?" Gracie asked.

"Thanks, no. I already had a piece of berry pie with lunch today. Did you see the For Sale sign on the lawn in front of the little house on the corner?" Edna asked.

"Yes, Rocko put it on the lawn on Saturday. You know, Mom—I saw the craziest thing happen over there. I was washing dishes, and I looked out the window and saw Rocko go to work. Not ten minutes after his car pulled out of the driveway, a huge van—the biggest I have ever seen—pulled in front of the house. Six guys went into the house and started putting things in the van. By one o'clock, the van drove away. Ann and their three boys got into the car and left too. At five thirty Rocko pulled into the driveway, went into the house, and in about three minutes he came running out of the house and jumped into his car, backed up, and peeled out, burning rubber all the way down the street. Ann must have packed up and left, and Rocko had no idea until he got home. I'll know more when Carla comes back from vacation. Ann and Carla are friends."

"He must have done something to make her really mad," Edna said.

"They always seemed happy. They came to several of our block parties, and they seemed fine," Gracie said.

"Gracie, I called the real estate company and asked how much they're asking for the house; the house is only three years old, and they want $21,500, two thousand dollars down, and a five-and-a-quarter-percent loan. That's a very good price. I was thinking you and Billy should buy it."

"What? We have no money. We can't afford two thousand down on a house," Gracie said.

"William sold a piece of the farm and sent me half the money. I can give you the down payment. The money should be yours anyway."

"Oh, Mom, that would be wonderful. I can't believe it. I watched that house being built, and I love it. Ann is super clean, and even with three kids her house was always spotless. They put in a great flower garden, and there are about ten rose bushes in the front, and four in the back."

"You talk to Billy about it, and I'll call and make an appointment with the real estate agent," Edna said.

Later that night:

Gracie walked into the bedroom and found Billy sitting on the edge of the bed staring at the wall. Surprised, she asked, "Are you upset at me for asking you if we could buy the Maronis' house?" Gracie asked.

"No, not mad exactly," Billy answered.

Gracie sat next him on the bed. "What is it? You look very unhappy."

Billy turned and looked at Gracie. "I don't understand why Edna would just give us two thousand dollars. That's a lot of money. Besides, doesn't she think I can take care of my family?"

"Of course she does. She brags about all your promotions and tells everyone about how smart you are," Gracie said.

"Maybe she does it to try to buy our love," Billy said suspiciously.

"Absolutely not; she does it because she cares about us. She would rather see us happily living in that house than use the money for herself. If we're happy, she's happy. That's who she is. There is not a single selfish bone in her body. She loves us. That's the only reason she offered us the money," Gracie said as she left the room and slammed the door on her way out.

A few minutes later Billy came out of the bedroom and looked around the house for Gracie, but she wasn't there. He opened the front door, walked out onto the little entryway, and saw her sitting in the car.

He opened the car door and got in. "I'm sorry, you have to understand that I have a hard time trusting people, or trusting that someone would love me so much that they would put me before themselves. Please call your mom and tell her to set up the appointment for us to see the house. We already know the house, and it's perfect for us, right?"

Turning around in the seat, she threw her arms around Billy and kissed him all over his face and neck. "Thank you"—smack—"Thank you"—smack—"Thank you!"

Chapter 47

Friday, October 25, 1966

Billy answered the ringing phone. "Hello."

"You'll never guess what Mom is doing this weekend," Gracie said on the other end of the line.

"Going riding on that guy's motorcycle again," Billy said, teasing.

"No! She isn't seeing that guy anymore. Remember Bob, that man she met at the singles' group? They're going to Las Vegas to get married."

"What?" Billy said.

"Yes, she just called me. She said he's a nice guy, a widower with his own home, and he's an accountant that works for Lockheed. She said that when he asked her to marry him, she couldn't think of any reason not to say yes."

"It sure is fast," Billy said.

"I know. I hope she'll be happy. She deserves to have someone nice," Gracie said.

"Are you upset that she didn't tell you about him sooner?"

"No, he sounds like a better match for her that the guy on the motorcycle," Gracie said sarcastically, "But I am surprised she didn't let us get to know him before she ran off and married him. I knew something was up because she hasn't called me or come around to see the kids much since she helped us buy the house."

"Your feelings are hurt," Billy stated.

"No, it just makes me sad. I thought she would be more excited about the house. I wanted her to be excited too . . . well, yes, maybe my feelings are hurt a little," Gracie said. "I just don't understand, and the kids miss having her around."

"Now don't be such a mama's girl. Your mom deserves to have a better life with some fun after William," Billy said with a little laughter in his voice. "Oh, by the way, I was going to call you, but you beat me to it. John and Dick said they would help us move the furniture on Saturday. Do you have everything packed yet?"

"Yes, while the kids were taking their nap, I took a lot of boxes to the house. I emptied all the boxes with kitchen stuff and some of the things that went in our closets. It was great that I didn't have to do any cleaning at all. Ann kept the house so spotlessly clean there was nothing to do. Even the shelves in the kitchen were already lined and everything."

"Good, it shouldn't be too hard to move the rest of our things. I'm sure the neighbors will help. I have to go back to work. I'll see you at five," Billy said.

Gracie and Billy's Home
Stockton Street,
San Jose
March 26, 1967

"Mommy, why do me and Scottie have to sit here on the sofa?" Mary asked.

"Daddy's hiding the Easter eggs. He's almost finished. You like finding Easter eggs, don't you?" Gracie asked.

"What about Tommy? He's too little to find any eggs. Maybe I can find some for him," Mary said.

"That's a good girl. You help him, and you can keep the eggs. Where is Kris?" Gracie asked.

"I don't know," Mary said.

Gracie walked down the hall and called out, "Kris, where are you?" There was no answer. "Krrrris, Krrris," she called.

Gracie opened the front door and looked out. There on the porch Kris sat quietly stacking little rocks into columns.

"Kris, come inside. We're almost ready to search for the Easter eggs. You can show Scottie how to find the eggs. He doesn't know how."

The small towheaded girl jumped up and took her mother's hand. "I know how; Daddy told me how. He said to look under bushes and dark places."

"Okay, you kids, come and find the eggs," Billy called from the sliding back door.

"Oh boy," Mary yelled. "Put Tommy on the grass, and I'll put some eggs in his basket."

"Yeah, like he's going to sit still on the lawn," Gracie said under her breath. She let go of Kris's hand and picked up the baby that sat in the playpen by the opened door leading to the backyard.

"Come on, Kris, let's go out," Gracie said. "Mary, where did Scottie go? I don't see him."

"He's already outside with Daddy," Mary answered.

"That little dickens sure is fast," Gracie said, smiling.

Billy and Gracie sat at the picnic table while three of their children ran around the yard looking for Easter eggs. The youngest, Tommy, not yet a year old, sat in the middle of the yard on the grass looking around at the others as if thinking, "What the heck is going on?"

"Mom, Scottie took the one I found for Tommy," Mary squealed.

"Scottie, give the blue one back to Mary," Billy said.

"It's mine," Scottie cried.

"No, it's mine," Mary cried.

Gracie got up from the table, turned to Billy, and with a smile said, "I'm leaving this argument to you. I'm gonna go check on the ham that's in the oven."

When dinner was ready, Gracie set the ham in the middle of the table with the mashed potatoes, biscuits, gravy, green beans, and sliced tomatoes. She walked over to the window and watched Billy help the kids sort through their baskets of colored Easter eggs. There they were—her beautiful family, in the beautifully flowered backyard, of her very own home. Noting the pleasing picture it made, she said with a sigh, "How can I be any happier than I am right now?"

Chapter 48

Saturday May 24, 1968

Driving slowly down Stockton Street, Gracie was lost in thought, trying to figure out why she'd felt so uneasy at home the last few days. She knew something was wrong; something was different.

Pulling into the driveway, she saw Billy, his shirt off, digging the weeds out of the rose garden. He looked up. She waved. He waved back.

Removing the groceries from the backseat of the car, she turned and walked toward the house. "Do you need any help?" Billy yelled.

"No, I have everything. Dinner will be ready in about an hour," Gracie said.

"What are we having?" Billy called.

"Swiss steak and corn on the cob," Gracie said.

"Great!" Billy said.

Walking into the house, she checked on the children in the backyard before setting the grocery bags on the table. "One, two, three, four—yes they're all there," she mumbled to herself. Seeing her kids running around playing, she smiled.

After setting the bags on the table, she turned and looked in the living room. A chill crept up her back. Gracie thought, God, something is awfully wrong. Where is this feeling coming from? Slowly she wandered into the living room, and her whole body started shaking. The closer she got to the sofa, the harder her body reacted. She got down on her hands and knees and looked under the sofa.

Looking up, she could see a tear in the fabric underneath. She reached in and touched something that felt like paper, then grabbed it. She pulled out four magazines. As she got back up on her feet and looked through the stack, she thought she was going to faint. She collapsed on the sofa. In her hands were magazines, and on the covers were pictures of fully naked men, their genitals prominently exposed.

Billy walked in the door, obviously shocked at what he saw. "What are you doing?" he said, irritated.

"What are you doing hiding this in our home?" Gracie said, throwing the magazines at Billy and stomping off into the bedroom and slamming the door.

Billy opened the bedroom door and walked in slowly.

Gracie sat on the edge of the bed with her head in her hands, crying softly. She thought about Ty's warning that day a long time ago, and how right he had been about Billy being gay. The more she thought about this, and about how her life and family would never be the same again, she begin to sob hysterically. The pain from this realization and disappointment was almost unbearable.

"Gracie, it's not what you think," Billy begged.

"I don't want to hear it, Billy. I know what they are, but I can't believe you brought them home. Ty was right, wasn't he? You are gay, and there is nothing we can do about it," she yelled.

"Gracie, I gave a guy from work a ride home, and he left them in my car. I didn't want the kids to see them, so I hid them until Monday, when I can give them back to him," Billy said dramatically.

"Sure, I'll be stupid enough to believe that," Gracie said through her tears. "I will never believe that lie. I hate this, and I hate that you are lying to me again. Why don't you just go be with your gay friends and keep this out of our home?" she yelled as she grabbed a bunch of coat hangers lying on the bed and flung them at Billy.

"Don't throw things at me. I'm telling you the truth," Billy yelled.

"Damn you!" Gracie yelled as she picked up a dish from the dresser and threw it at him.

Billy grabbed her arm and pushed her up against the wall. "Don't be a bitch. You don't know anything. I didn't do this on purpose," Billy yelled louder. Surprised at the depth of his own anger, he backed up a little, still holding her, and said, "I'm sorry. I'm sorry. You must believe me." Suddenly he let her go and left the bedroom. "We'll talk about this later when you calm down."

"I can't believe that after all the lies I've told, now that I am telling her the truth she won't believe me. I wouldn't bring these books into our home on purpose. I would never let the kids see these," Billy muttered as he picked up the magazines from the living room floor and walked out the front door. Getting into his car he hit the steering wheel will his clenched fist, "Damn, I need to talk to her." Starting the car, he backed out of the driveway and sped down Stokes Street.

Gracie heard the kids coming in the sliding back door. Quickly she hurried into the bathroom, washed her face, and brushed her hair.

Going into the kitchen, she smiled at the children looking into the grocery bags checking to see if mom bought some treats.

"Okay, there is nothing in there you'll like. As soon as I put the groceries away, I'll make dinner. Kris, go turn on the TV. I know there must be cartoons for you guys to watch until dinner is ready. Boys, go wash your hands and please do it quietly."

As Gracie placed the tuna casserole in the oven there was a loud noise coming from the living room.

Mary called out, "Mommy, Tommy fell and hit is head on the table."

Rushing into the living room, Gracie picked up the baby and hurried into the bathroom. Tommy was still screaming as Gracie placed a cold cloth on his head. "Shh, shh, it's alright there's no bump. It's okay, it just scared you. I'm scared too baby," Gracie said as her tears ran down her cheeks onto the soft blond hair of her toddler.

Sunday, July 14, 1968

Billy sat on the front porch step admiring the perfectly trimmed lawn, the colorful rose garden, and the flowerbeds with their living bouquet of flowers. This was his creation, and he didn't want to leave it, but most of all he didn't want to leave his children.

I must make her understand. I hope at least she'll listen to my plan and give it a chance. My idea will work if she is willing to try it, but if she doesn't, I'll have to leave again. It will devastate her. The way our life is now will not work anymore. I can't stop being uptight and angry all the time. It's affecting the kids. It's not going to change as long as things stay the way they are now. As long as I keep lying about who I am, I will never be happy, Billy thought as he held his hands tightly to stop them from shaking.

Gracie stood at the window by the front door and watched Billy pull flowers from the Acacia tree, and then crush them in his fist before tossing them into the flowerbed.

This is not going to be good, she thought.

She opened the door and went onto the porch. "The kids are in bed. Do you still want to talk to me?"

"Yes, do you want me to go in and get you a kitchen chair to sit in?" Billy asked.

"No, I'll sit here beside you if it's okay," Gracie said.

"It's okay."

Not looking at Gracie, Billy said, "While you and the kids were in Missouri, I went to gay bars a lot. I went before that, but while you were gone, I went almost every night. I couldn't seem to stay away. It was the first time in a very long time that I felt like myself, like the person I'm supposed to be. I don't want to lie to you about it anymore. Gracie, I think I'm gay. No, no, I now know that I'm gay. I need to stop fighting it and accept what I am. You said you're more self-aware and happier than you've been in years since you've been going to the self-awareness classes. I want that too. Do you understand?"

"Did you bring anyone home?" Gracie asked quietly.

"I didn't sleep with anyone, and I didn't bring anyone home—not that I didn't want to. I just didn't." Tom's face flashed in his mind, but he shook his head to make it go away. "I want you to consider something that I think will work for us. Now, please try to understand and consider this, okay?" Billy pleaded.

The seriousness of his tone made Gracie turn and look at him. To her surprise, his eyes glistened with what looked like the beginning of tears.

"I know several couples that are living happily with the husband's gay lifestyle and the wife accepting it. They live normally in every way except the husband goes out with his gay friends. I think we could be happier than we are now if you could accept that arrangement. I know I haven't been fair to you sexually, but you really haven't been fair to me either. You never bothered to ask me if I was happy with things the way they are. You just go on day to day as if our relationship is normal. You never asked or tried to find out. I can tell you, the way we live is not the way a normal married couple lives. If we tried this new acceptance, everything would be the same except I will be happier and not so uptight."

"What you just said isn't fair, Billy. I know things are not normal with us. I hear my girlfriends talk about how often they are intimate, and what they do in bed. I thought you didn't like sex with me, and I didn't know how to change it. I don't know anything about sex. Maybe we should have talked to each other about our needs. Honestly, no one ever talked to me about sex. Not even my doctors. When I had my first appointment with Dr. Cunningham, he asked me a bunch of questions, like 'How often are you and your husband intimate?' I wasn't sure what that meant, but I told him twice a month, even though that was a lie, I thought 'once in a while' wasn't a good answer. I noticed that he had a surprised look on his face, but I didn't know why until I listened to my friends' conversations about sex."

"I know, I know, you're naïve, and I should have probably done a better job at being a husband. Gracie, I'm homosexual—do you understand why I couldn't? I'm sorry for what I said. It's not all your fault," Billy said kindly.

"If you and I live together and you go out with your friends and have gay sex with other people, am I supposed to find a boyfriend or something?" Gracie asked.

"I don't know. I don't like the idea. You know I love you. I've always been afraid of you leaving me. I know that's why I was so reluctant to let you get your driver's license. I thought you might go out and find someone that would make you happy. It wasn't fair; I know that now. I've known about being gay for a long time, but I couldn't bring myself to say anything because I didn't want to leave, but also I didn't think you could handle all the kids by yourself. This has not been an easy decision."

"Knowing what I know now about how our life should be, what I desire so much is to have someone love me and be my friend too. I do need more than sex; sex is a natural desire, but you can't even seem to give me affection. How can I be your wife and stay home, clean house, and take care of the children with nothing else in my life, while you go out, have relationships, and be gay? No, I don't think so! If there's one thing I've learned in the self-awareness class, it's that I can be so much more than I have been in the past. I want to be more. I want to feel loved. You can't ask me to be here when you need a housewife and tell me I should look the other way when you want to be gay," Gracie said loudly.

"Shhhh. You'll wake the kids," Billy said. "Even if you don't believe me, I've felt more love for you than any other person in my life. I don't want to lose you. Will you please meet my friends Cody and Maria? They've been married for fifteen years. You'll see how happy they are, and how they make it work. I promise we can have our marriage and be happy too," he said, moving closer to her.

"I don't want to break up our family, but I don't think it will work," Gracie said.

"Just meet them, please," Billy asked.

"Okay, I'll meet them, but I don't promise anything. Right now I need to think, and I can't sleep in the same bed with you," Gracie said.

"I need my rest to go to work tomorrow. I need to sleep in the bed," Billy said.

Gracie stood up, opened the door, and said, "Okay, I'll sleep on the sofa."

Chapter 49

Sunday, July 28, 1968

"I hate it Billy. I can't do it," Gracie said as Billy drove the car back to their house. "What makes you think Maria is happy? I think she likes having a home, and she likes what Cody provides for her. All she talked about was how happy she is, and how it didn't bother her that her husband has boyfriends, as long as he doesn't have girlfriends. I don't believe her. She cares, I'm sure of it. I won't settle for a marriage like that. I don't know why I find it so terribly offensive. I really don't understand. All I know is that I will not live like that, pretending to be happy when I'm dying inside. You don't get it. I love you. I want to be with you, and I will be jealous, and I will feel bad, no matter whom you are with, whether it's a man or a woman. We both have lived a lie for far too long."

Friday, August 28, 1968

Sitting at the kitchen table Gracie thought about her life, her loneliness, and her need to have Billy stay home at night and help her with the children. She thought about the possible solution to her situation that came the day before when Carol told her she was going to ask Billy to move in with her while they sorted things out. When Gracie told her that she loved the idea, Carol offered to talk to Billy the next day.

"If he can't manage to stay home, he needs to move out. I hate watching him come and go without concern for the children or me. It's just too hard to take. I don't know why I'm sleeping on the couch when most nights he doesn't bother to come home until the morning anyway. I hate it. He doesn't realize how hard it is being separated and yet still living together," Gracie said loudly to an empty house.

Suddenly, the front door opened with a bang, boom, bang, boom as the children came bounding into the living room. Eight little arms were swinging, eight little legs running toward the kitchen. This was Gracie's cue that it was dinnertime. Still lamenting about why she couldn't seem to get herself together, she stood up slowly, let out a big sigh, and went to the kitchen counter.

Now that her kitchen was crowded with giggling, laughing, children, her mood started to change. Turning toward the noise, she smiled at the one thing in her life that was pure: her four sweet, funny, energetic children.

Opening the cupboard, she looked for something to prepare for dinner. What she found was an almost empty cabinet that provided few options. In her depression, she'd neglected to go shopping, and now all she had was peanut butter, jelly, tuna, and bread.

Gracie stood at her kitchen counter making the tuna sandwiches, her mind active with mundane thoughts of the groceries she needed to buy at the market on Saturday. These ordinary shopping ideas floated in and out of her mind without enthusiasm or exhilaration. Lately there was rote to her musing of chores, children, and her new job at the health clinic. Because of her fear of what lay ahead, she could only allow herself to think about her life one day at a time.

The newly purchased yellow wall phone rang loudly. Startled, Gracie dropped the tuna can in the kitchen sink. Recovering quickly, she turned on the water to rinse her hands, but before she could dry them the phone stopped ringing. "Darn it!" she said. Knowing how quiet and lonely her evening would be after she put the children to bed, she longed for conversation with an adult, any adult. The phone rang again, and abruptly she picked it up, damp hands and all.

Trying to sound cheerful and not let on that she was feeling lonely, she said brightly, "Hello."

Carol, returned with a "Hi, what'cha doing?"

Gracie didn't have time to answer before Carol said excitedly, "Hey, girl, you need to get out of the house. Find a babysitter. I'm taking you out dancing." And then she hung up abruptly.

"What the heck was that?" Gracie said as she dried the damp telephone with the dishcloth, shaking her head. "That Carol, what is she up to now?"

She placed the tuna, chips, and milk on the table. "I can't go out, I'm not divorced. I don't want to meet any men. And besides, I don't dance."

Walking to the end of the kitchen cabinet, Gracie looked into the mirror she had placed there the week before. "Look at me." She gasped. "I'm a mess. I can't possibly go out with my hair looking like this."

Minutes later Carol—a typical young, vibrant, confident female that the women's lib movement spawned in the late sixties—walked in the front door and into the kitchen. "Who were you talking to?" she asked. Gracie laughed and repeated the thoughts that she had shared with her mirror and added, "I really can't go out tonight. I just don't know who I can call to babysit."

A rapid knock on the front door startled the women. Carol walked through the living room and opened the door cautiously. On the doorstep, baby-faced sixteen-year-old Kathy from the house next door stood looking forlorn and dejected.

"My sister and I had a fight again, and I need to get out of the house. Can I babysit for you tonight, please? For free," she asked woefully.

Gracie turned to Carol and stared as if to accuse her of putting Kathy up to this, but Carol quickly shook her head and said, "I didn't do this."

Gracie mumbled, "Well, I guess." Looking at Kathy, she asked, "Did Carol call you?"

"No, honestly, I just want to get out of my house," Kathy said adamantly. Without further comment, Gracie turned and walked back into the kitchen.

Calling to the children, she said, "Please sit down at the table and eat; Mommy is going out with Aunt Carol for a while." Without questions, they noisily ran into the kitchen and found their place at the table.

Thirty minutes later, Gracie tucked the last little towhead under the covers, pulling the blanket under the tiny chin. I'm not sure this is the right thing to do, but I'm so lonely, and going out with Carol sounds like it might be fun.

Carol, standing in the doorway and seeing the worried look on Gracie's face, smiled and said, "Gracie, they'll be fine. We'll be back in two hours. I promise."

At about nine p.m., dressed in her best white pants and pink summer top, Gracie followed Carol out the front door and into her car.

Pulling out from the driveway, Carol stepped on the gas hard, and the little red sport car roared down the street.

"There are four or five different dance clubs around here, so we can be choosy," Carol said, laughing. Gracie stiffened at this announcement.

Shortly, the little red car pulled into the crowded parking lot of a dance club not more than a mile from Gracie's house. It was a busy place, and finding a parking space wasn't easy. Around and around the lot they drove, until, finally, someone pulled out of a parking spot and Carol pulled in. "Here we are," she said as she turned off the engine, reached around to the backseat, and hauled her large bulky handbag into her lap. Tilting the rearview mirror toward her face, she pulled out a compact and refreshed her makeup while Gracie watched.

The women got out and walked toward the club entrance. Carol strutted gracefully, as if she owned the world. Gracie, head down, followed close at her heels, feeling more afraid with every quick step.

Grace's gait slowed as she walked toward the bright lights coming through the entrance of the bar. Still afraid to lift her head completely, she raised her eyes to the left and noticed the silhouette of two men, one noticeably tall, standing just outside the entrance. She felt their stares as she produced her driver's license to the bouncer and he stamped her hand.

To Gracie's surprise, she and Carol walked straight through the room and into the restroom. As Carol removed her brush from her handbag, she explained, "There's a routine to going out to a dance club—it's called finding the right spot to look good and to have fun. The routine, at least for the women, is that we walk all the way through the club to the washroom while carefully examining the scene as we go by. We look to see if it's too crowded, if there are enough guys, if we like the music, and most importantly if this feels like the right place to meet someone and dance. While we're here, we comb our hair, freshen our lipstick, check for mascara smears, and last, but most important, a quick butt check in the mirror to make sure it looks appealing. And after all that, we make a decision whether to stay at this place or go to the next club."

While applying fresh mascara, Carol turned to Gracie and said, "Were not staying here. It's too crowded."

Feeling uncomfortable and wanting to leave, Gracie said, "Okay."

Leaving the washroom, her eyes glued to the floor, Gracie managed to fight her way through the crowded bar while staying only a couple of inches from Carol's back.

A few minutes after leaving the parking lot, Gracie said quietly, "Carol, I don't think I'm ready to be in the singles' scene. I think you should take me home."

"Too late, we're here," Carol said as she pulled into the next parking lot.

Gracie spoke louder and with determination. "Carol, It won't be much fun for you having me hanging around when all I'm going to do is sit and watch. I don't want to talk to any guys, and I sure don't want to dance—do you understand?"

Ignoring again, Carol opened her car door, quickly got out, and hurried toward the entrance of the second club without saying a word to Gracie.

Gracie thought for a minute about just waiting in the car, but suddenly jumped out and ran to catch up with Carol.

As Gracie passed through dim light of the second club's entrance, she noticed to her surprise that there was another very tall man standing inconspicuously in the shadows watching her enter.

Again they walked through the club, went to the washroom, and primped. And as before, Carol decided this wasn't the right place to have fun and walked out. Gracie found herself back in Carol's car proceeding to the next bar.

The fourth club was the Adriatic, the biggest and most popular dance club in San Jose. With her head lowered less than before, Gracie held out her hand for the bouncer's stamp. In a cheerful, flirty voice, he told her to have a good time. She looked up, blushed, and gave him a shy smile. As she continued into the bar, she saw the two men—the tall one was standing against the wall near the entrance. A light shone directly on the tall man, and Gracie could see that he was handsome and had a nice smile.

Upon entering the club, Gracie marveled at the size of this room with its grand raised stage and the rock band playing with gusto. Many couples danced, while others sat at small round tables engrossed in conversation, or just listened to the music.

Carol found a small round table with two chairs and set her purse on one, leaving the second chair for Gracie. Walking toward the stage, Carol turn toward Gracie and said, "They're playing my song."

Gracie sat down and watched as Carol found a dance partner near the stage. They seemed be talking happily to each other as they went onto the dance floor and moved as if they had been dancing together for years.

The room was comfortable, and the band was amazing, so Gracie let herself relax and feel energy. This isn't so bad, as long as no one asks me to dance, she thought.

Before they left the house, she mentioned to Carol that she didn't have much money, and her reply was, "If you have a dollar to buy one glass of wine, you'll be set. You're pretty; I know there will be men offering to buy you a drink."

When the waitress came to the table and asked Gracie what she wanted to drink, she thought of Carol's advice and smiled. "I'll have a glass of white wine please."

When the waitress returned with the wine and set it on the table, she said, "That will be one dollar." Gracie removed one of the two dollars she had in her purse and paid for the wine. Having no experience in buying a drink for herself, she didn't give the waitress a tip. The waitress smiled and walked away, giving no indication that she was slighted.

Gracie felt his presence at her back before he said, "Do you want to dance?"

Turning around, she looked up and found herself staring straight into a man's waistline, right above the belt at the shirt buttons just above the buckle.

She slowly looked upward into his face. Her startled expression revealed her recognition of just who this was asking her to dance. Because of his height, and the seeing him at the entrance of this club, she knew that this was the man she saw at the door of every club they had walked into.

His laughing eyes sparkled with delight at Gracie's obvious recognition.

Again, he asked, "Would you like to dance?"

Forgetting for the moment that she didn't dance, Gracie said, "Okay."

He held her hand softly, his arm tight around her waist, and looked down at her. "I'm Steve."

Gracie moved awkwardly on her tiptoes. "I'm Gracie."

They danced to "By the Time I Get to Phoenix." He led, and she followed the best she could. They didn't talk. Gracie's relaxed and placed her cheek on his chest, and noticed that it felt very good. When the music stopped, Gracie said, "Thank you," and walked back to the table.

In a cheerful voice, while pulling out the chair next to her, he asked, "Do you mind if I sit and talk to you?" Not waiting for her to answer, he removed Carol's purse from the chair and sat down. Gracie blushed, and her ears became hot.

"You are so pretty. I had to follow you. You know I followed you, right?" Steve said, smiling.

"What do you mean?" Gracie asked.

"My buddy and I were standing by the door at The Board Room, and when I saw you go in, I waited while you and your friend went into the bathroom. I was surprised that you walked out so soon. We hurried out, ran across the parking lot, and got behind your friend's car so I could follow. We did this every time you and your friend went in and came out again. I was worried I would run out of gas before you stayed in one place," Steven said with a grin.

"I'm glad she decided to stay here. I was beginning to wonder if going from place to place was all we were going to do," Gracie said smiling.

"Me too," Steven said, taking Gracie's hand, "Tell me about yourself."

Maybe it was the wine, or Steven's smiling eyes, but Gracie found herself talking to him openly about Billy, her four kids.

When she finished talking Steven asked, "Is it possible for me to meet your four kids?"

Surprised, Gracie, stuttered, "Yes, uh yes, that would be okay."

Gracie's heart was beating so fast and loudly from the thought of this, she was sure Steven could hear it.

"Give me your phone number and I'll call so I can meet your kids. Okay?"

Gracie and Steven didn't dance again, but talked about their lives. Steven talked about being in the Navy for four years and having only recently returned home for good, while Gracie talked about the children and trying to figure out what to do next. At midnight, Carol came to the table to say she was ready to leave.

Steve walked Gracie to the car, gave her a hug and a kiss on the cheek, and said, "I'll call you soon."

Gracie looked at the clock on the living room wall. One a.m.! When was the last time I stayed up until one?, she thought.

Leaning down to smooth the blankets on the sofa that was to be her bed for another night, Gracie thought of Steve and smiled.

"He really didn't seem to mind when I told him that I had kids. I hope he calls me, but I'll have to tell him that he can't come here or meet the kids as long as Billy lives here," she said to the empty room.

"Damn!" she said suddenly as she thought of Billy and his disrespect for her feelings.

Standing up quickly, she looked down at her sofa bed and said loudly, "No! I will not sleep here another night. I've given Billy enough time to find a place. I can't live like this any longer. He isn't respecting the kids or me. I need to move on."

Gracie turned and walked down the hall to the bedroom, went to Billy's closet, and methodically removed his starched white shirts, his finely pressed business suits, his underwear, socks, shampoo, razor, and toothbrush. Carefully folding the clothes, she placed everything neatly into two suitcases.

Tears wet her cheek as she looked around the bedroom for Billy's personal articles. She cried for the loss of her marriage, her children's father, her husband, and the future they wouldn't share.

Taking a black-and-white framed picture of the two of them from the dresser, she sat on the edge of the bed and stared at Billy's image. "You know I have to do this, not because I think you are a bad man but just a man that has experienced so many bad things. The bad things in your life are the cause and effect of this family having to pay the excruciating high price of not having you in our life. If you are gay or straight it doesn't matter now, but the people that damaged you are the ones to blame for your confusion. Maybe if I wasn't so immature I could have made a difference in how you felt. I know I wasn't the best wife for you. I'm so sorry that I'm not able to do what you want me to do to keep all of us together." She held the photo close to her chest and began to sob.

After a few minutes, she rose from the bed, composed herself, and went into the bathroom. She grabbed some tissue and blew her nose, then picked up a washcloth and scrubbed her mascara-blackened cheeks with soap and hot water.

Looking in the mirror, she said, "Oh damn, the kids better not wake up and see me like this; I'm a mess." Gracie moved the suitcases into the kitchen and set them near the table that held a pen and a writing tablet.

Gracie went over to the wall phone near the sink, picked up the receiver, and called Carol.

"I'm sorry to call you this late," she began, and continued to explained to Carol what she was doing and hoped it was okay that she was sending Billy to her apartment at whatever time he decided to come home. "For once I must be strong and not let my feelings stop me from doing what I must do. I must push him into moving on because what he's doing now is hurting all of us."

After hanging up the phone, she went to the table, sat down, picked up the pen, and began to write.

Billy,

I refuse to live like this any longer. Living separately in the same house is too hard. I can't continue this arrangement. You don't come home until two a.m. every night, if you come home at all. Meanwhile I'm sleeping on the sofa. I feel like you are punishing me for not agreeing to go along with your plan.

Well, if you are, it's working, because it does hurt me to know what you are doing while I am home taking care of the family. What am I supposed to tell the kids when they see this happening? They feel confused when they see you come home at seven in the morning, change your clothes, and leave for work without saying anything to them. They are sad, and they need you to tell them that everything is going to be okay. You are punishing them as much as you are punishing me, and they did nothing wrong.

I'm so upset with you that I can't have you living here even one more day. I put a dead bolt on the door this morning and packed your suitcases with everything you will need for a week. Carol knows we are having problems and offered to have you stay with her as long as you wanted. You can come get the rest of your things when I'm not home. Call and we can arrange it. I'm sorry. Maybe later when it doesn't hurt so much we can be friends. I hope we can, because no matter what, I love you, and you will always be the kids' father.

Gracie picked up the note, walked to the front door, and went out onto the porch. She taped the note on the door and placed the two suitcases away from the porch light near the acacia tree.

She went back into the house, walked to their bedroom, turned out the light, crawled into her king-size bed, and pulled the covers up to her chin. She closed her eyes and murmured, "I'm so scared, oh, God, I'm so scared. Our Father, which art in heaven . . ."

Chapter 50

Friday, October 25, 1968

"Hey, Billy, you busy?" Jake said, knocking on the door frame as he walked into Billy's office.

"Hi, Jake, you're back in town! How's the job in San Francisco going?" Billy said.

"Yeah, I'm here for the weekend. I love it. Too many men, not enough time," Jake said, laughing.

"I'd like to transfer to the office there. I'm tired of San Jose and the scene here," Billy said.

"I heard you and Gracie are not together now," Jake said.

"I told her that I'm gay, and she kicked me out. I wanted us to stay together in an arrangement like Cody and Marie have. I spent a lot of time trying to figure out a way we could keep our family together, and she wouldn't even consider it."

"Wow, when did all this happen?"

"About eight weeks ago."

"Where are you living? What are you going to do?" Jake asked.

"I stayed with my sister for a couple of weeks, and now I'm staying with Tom. I plan on getting my own place soon. Gracie wants a divorce. I was a jerk for a while. Well, if I'm really truthful, I haven't been exactly nice the last few months. I don't know what's wrong with me. Even now, I'm not being a dad; I hate being away from the kids, but I can't seem to go back to the house. It hurts. I've failed everyone. Gracie already has a new boyfriend, and it feels awful to know he is spending time with my kids," Billy said, hanging his head.

"Already, a boyfriend? That seems fast," Jake said.

"I guess she's been lonely for a long time."

"Not any lonelier than you. You are a gay man trying to be straight. That could drive you crazy. But not anymore— you can be yourself now! I came down to San Jose to hit the bars tonight and catch up with some of my old flames," Jake said, sliding his hand across Billy's shoulders teasingly.

Billy removed Jake's hand from his shoulder gently and laughed. "I'm not your flame, but you're right, I've been feeling sorry for myself for too long, so let's do it. I'll be finished here at five. Let's get something to eat, and then go to The Tinkers Bar. It's been too long since I've danced."

Epilogue

Billy

Billy eventually did move to San Francisco when Castle and Cook promoted him into the Foreign Sales Tax Department. He was happy living in the city. Now he could finally be himself and not worry about people finding out that he was gay. He found fulfillment in the music, the art, and the eclectic lifestyle of his San Francisco friends.

Unfortunately his ideal life in the city became a terrible challenge when the AIDS epidemic hit the gay community. Many of his friends died of AIDS. When longtime friend Jake lost his life to AIDS and passed away Billy was devastated.

After spending too many days and nights at the bedside of dying friends, Billy decided that San Francisco was too sad and dangerous so in the Summer of 1987 he moved back home to Missouri.

The move to Missouri proved to be even more depressing for the now anxiety-ridden Billy. Everything he tried to do to improve his life fell apart. He bought a little land about five miles from Garberville and hired a local contractor to build a house. The contractor was a crook. He built a substandard home and stole the money Billy gave him to pay for the building supplies.

Billy's retirement money soon ran out and he needed to find work. Because of depression and anxiety he didn't want to try to be an accountant or work in an office. He didn't think he could deal with the stress. He found a job as an entrance guard for a small company on the outskirts of town. It turned out to be just the kind of job he needed. He had no interaction with company employees other than to wave or say hello as they drove through the gate going to work.

Billy filled his hermit-like life with his favorite animals like chickens, ducks, donkeys, goats, and peacocks. He named every one, and they followed him around like pets. His children called him Dr. Doolittle of Missouri.

He spent very little time with his family and rarely contacted his children. With his anxiety issues he found it easier to have the children contact him and make the effort to visit. His mother passed away from diabetes. His stepfather and two brothers passed away, each from a separate unfortunate circumstance. His beloved grandmother passed away very soon after his grandfather.

Carol moved back to Missouri a few years before her mother passed away. She reached out to Billy, but for reasons known only to him, he rejected her.

When Billy's anxiety became debilitating he went to his physician and asked for help. The physician prescribed an anxiety medication that seemed to help. He called Gracie before Thanksgiving in 2000 to talk about making a trip to California. He wanted to visit his children and meet his six grandchildren.

Gracie encouraged him to come, telling him that she would find him a motel close to her house, and that she and her husband would be there to help him get around.

Although he was anxious he enjoyed his time with the family immensely. Later he told Gracie that even though he enjoyed being with the children and grandchildren it was a difficult trip. He said that he probably wouldn't be able to come to California again.

Billy became friends with Hank, a young family man who lived on a nearby farm. Billy and Hank shared a fascination with chicken husbandry. They became partners in an effort to develop a new variety of chickens.

On a chilly morning in October, the local mail truck pulled up to the mailbox on the side of the road near Billy's house. Placing the day's mail in the box the postman saw that Billy hadn't picked up his mail for several days. He backed up and pulled into the driveway and saw that the door to Billy's house was slightly open and that the donkeys and goats in the barnyard were all moving anxiously around the feeding trough by the fence as if they were hungry. He heard loud clucking and sounds of distress coming from the nearby chicken house. Fearing the worst the postman called the sheriff's office as soon as he returned to the post office.

On October 11, 2009, the sheriff found that Billy had passed away in his bed. The coroner's report stated that Billy's passing was from arteriosclerosis (hardening of the arteries), which may have cause a stroke or heart attack. He was sixty-eight years old.

This is not the end of Billy's story. It continues with his children, grandchildren, and great-grandchildren.

Gracie

To Gracie's surprise Steven came to her house to meet the children the day after they met. Their relationship lasted for five years before he begin to feel restless and needed to move on to a different lifestyle. He told Gracie that he loved her and the children, but needed to explore other opportunities and travel the world. He felt that it wouldn't be fair to keep the little family hanging on when he couldn't see them being a part of his future. Gracie accepted his honesty as being kind.

Although the breakup devastated Gracie she didn't let the children or any of her friends know the depth of her pain. When she needed to cry, she cried late at night in her room, making sure the children didn't hear.

Gracie was working as a receptionist at a health clinic in April, 1970 when two year old Tommy broke his femur bone on the playground at school and required hospitalization. After a month in the hospital he returned home in a half-body cast. Gracie hired an older woman to care for Tommy while she was at work. One afternoon Gracie came home from work early and found Tommy in a dirty diaper that apparently hadn't been changed all day. She fired the woman on the spot. After a week of no luck in finding a replacement babysitter Gracie quit her job and signed up for welfare. Her children needed her.

In September, 1973 Silicon Valley was in its infancy when Gracie was fortunate to land a job in quality control at a start-up microelectronics manufacturing company. She became proficient at this job and went on to build a career as a quality assurance engineer for a major Silicon Valley company. She traveled the United States and Great Britain to audit manufacturing facilities and evaluate products made for highly classified projects.

Gracie met Samuel, a business owner and musician, in 1977. They fell in love quickly and bought a home together soon after they met. The rush to build a life together didn't work, and they separated after a month. Their on again, off again relationship continued for ten years until finally it was obvious that they should be together and were married in 1987. By this time Gracie's children had children of their own and Samuel transitioned easily into his role as father and grandfather. On September 2015 they celebrated twenty-eight years of marriage.